The Last of Sir Lancelot

The Last of Sir Lancelot

Richard Gordon

ROBERT HALE · LONDON

ISBN 0 7090 6422 5

Robert Hale Limited
Clerkenwell House
Clerkenwell Green
London EC1R 0HT

2 4 6 8 10 9 7 5 3 1

Typeset in North Wales by
Derek Doyle & Associates, Mold, Flintshire.
Printed in Great Britain by
St Edmundsbury Press, Bury St Edmunds, Suffolk.
Bound by WBC Book Manufacturers Limited, Bridgend.

Author's Note

The Placenta Drug Company, and its product
Sumo, do not exist.

1

'COME!' BARKED MR HUGO Lancelot Spratt, FRCS, consultant surgeon at St Swithin's Hospital in the City of London, in a manner genetically transmitted from his deceased surgical grandfather, Sir Lancelot Spratt.

'Oh, it's only you,' Hugo added, with obvious disrelish, as the door opened.

'Hello, darling,' said Dr Amanda Crockett-Jones, FRCA, consultant anaesthetist at Sir Swithin's Hospital and Chair of Women Homologously Associated with Medical Sciences (WHAMS).

'I wish you wouldn't call me "darling". You know how it irritates me.'

'That's why I do it, darling.'

She sat perkily on a bright blue plastic chair wedged against the small desk piled with neat stacks of medical journals and case-notes, in a tiny, white-walled ground-floor office of the Dickens surgical building.

'I suppose if you don't call me "darling" in the operating theatre, I should be sincerely grateful,' he said grumpily.

'What a dreadful suggestion! It would be all over the

hospital in no time, another war-cry of male surgeons in their degrading battle against female surgeons.'

'I am not aware of any such conflict.'

'Oh, darling, you do talk balls,' she said resignedly. 'How many female consultant surgeons are there on the staff of St Swithin's?'

'None, admittedly,' Hugo said firmly. 'That's only because none who were good enough ever applied for the job.'

'When you got on the staff here yourself two years ago, you beat one woman who'd won the Lister Prize and another who'd written a book on theories of pancreatitis.'

'They weren't as good as me at sewing,' he added, laughing.

'I do wish you wouldn't make stupid jokes outside the theatre, where they at least distract attention from your getting into difficulties.'

'What have you come about, anyway?'

'The memorial to Sir Lancelot.'

'Ah,' said Hugo.

Amanda was auburn-haired, short, slim, stylishly Armani suited, with the look of a determined elf. Her large brown eyes under arched eyebrows had, over her surgical mask, shattered her generation of male surgeons. Both the consultants were in their mid-thirties. She had achieved the premature eminence of an appointment to the staff of St Swithin's, Hugo considered, not through her acknowledged academic brilliance, but by her dynamic pushiness and the shortage on the professional ground of anaesthetists.

When conversing with Amanda he often regretted that he did not resemble his grandfather, whose portrait hung proudly in his double-glazed Dulwich home in south London. It was the depiction of Sir Lancelot Spratt in his prime, big and burly, fearsome-faced, battlingly bearded, attired always in black jacket and striped trousers, as correctly as lawyers and butlers. Though Hugo remembered him only in the tweeds of retirement, an agreeably waffly old soul, enjoying with Waltonian serenity the fishing-season.

Sir Lancelot kept a tackled-up rod in his hall; he could spot a rising trout from his bedroom window, and could catch it for breakfast. He had settled in his fifteenth-century house looking south across the delightful river Kennet in rolling Berkshire, built round a cosy courtyard – the original form of central heating, Sir Lancelot would joke, as it once contained the single log fire, and fireplaces were invented later. What more reposeful replacement for a life of busily cutting people to bits? he would ask schoolboy Hugo, to whom he was unfailingly generous, even by bequest with the vintage port. In the mayfly season, thirty summers ago, Sir Lancelot had hooked a huge trout from the mill pool and dropped dead on the bank. Probably from surprise, Hugo decided.

Hugo himself was fair haired, pink-faced, slight and handsome. He was president of the St Swithin's Medical School Drama Society, in the productions of which he regularly played the lead. These parts presented no difficulties to land, as he was a hospital consultant and the students would shortly require hospital jobs. He was at present rehearsing the role of Hamlet, which he felt as exciting a challenge as some of his surgery.

Like Sir Lancelot, Hugo wore a beard, which he had grown the previous year for King Lear, and which his wife condemned as ticklish, his secretary as unsightly, and his theatre nursing superintendent as insanitary. He felt stubbornly that a short beard would be commendably innovative in the new role, if not ventured by such models as Irving, Olivier and Gielgud. Hugo wore his Savile Row suit, as he was seeing a private patient later that May morning.

'You know I'm planning a statue of Sir Lancelot?' he reminded Amanda.

'You realize that idea is ridiculously ostentatious?'

'You could have said the same about putting Nelson on his column.'

'Nobody has a statue these days. Not even self-important politicians and terrifying generals. Why, a statue would cost as much as an entire new surgical suite, at today's chipping prices. Anyway, a modern sculptor would make him look like a deformed foetus in a bottle.'

'I rather thought his own statue would go nicely between the eighteenth-century surgeon and nineteenth-century physician we already have there,' Hugo said lamely. The annoyance of Amanda's persistent arguments was their lying unuttered in his own mind. 'But one statue per century is hardly an extravagance for an institution like St Swithin's, which has been operative over eight of them.'

'How do you suppose it would go over with the Minister of

Health? Why, they're already looking for any excuse they can grab to shut the hospital down as redundant. The only thing they're frightened about is public opinion. Which regards us as a St Paul's among the temples of healing, bless them.'

'They can't shut St Swithin's down! They *can't*,' cried Hugo with sudden ferocity, banging the desk with his fist.

'They can,' she assured him.

The government's resolve to abolish St Swithin's Hospital beside the Thames, as no longer necessary for the national health, had provoked among its staff and alumni outrage, anger, dismay, frustration and simple bafflement. The government might, with equal wisdom, have decided to demolish the nearby Tower of London as being no longer necessary for the national defence.

St Swithin's was founded by the Crusader King, Richard I, the Lion Heart, during one of his infrequent visits to his own kingdom, in March 1194. It was a gesture of gratitude to his generous subjects for raising the vast ransom of 150,000 marks to release him from imprisonment by the Holy Roman Emperor. The *Coeur de Lion* had unfortunately been seized near Vienna, while homecoming in plainly ineffective disguise, which had been necessitated by an inconvenient shipwreck in the Adriatic after gloriously defeating the Sultan Saladin under the walls of Jaffa. It was a story which Hugo had researched, being compulsively interested in the hospital's history, in which he considered his grandfather a shining item. Now the Minister of Health, the chicken-heart, Hugo could complain, planned ingloriously to flush down the fiscal drain this regal gift, scraping the national bedpan to smell out funds for our rapacious National Health Service.

'Why, it would be the equivalent of shutting down Balliol and Christ Church on the Isis, and King's and Trinity on the Cam.'

'Not to mention the London School of Economics. Quite so. But the National Health Service exists to keep the nation healthy, more or less, and London is cluttered with classy historic hospitals. This expensive decoration of yours would simply be publicized by the ministry as a selfish monstrosity, even if you recalled Michelangelo to knock it up. Who *is* going to pay for it, anyway?' she wondered suddenly. 'You can't expect a penny from the National Health, the National Heritage or the National Lottery.'

'I've a reasonably opulent friend or two in the City,' he said vaguely. These unwelcome remarks of hers, he had honestly to admit, he had himself entertained inwardly. 'I've planned a fund, inviting subscriptions in his memory.'

'But who remembers him?'

'Well, he discovered Spratt's gutter in the abdomen.'

'Whoever mentions Spratt's gutter today? It went out of surgery with the floating kidney.'

'True,' he admitted. 'But he *should* be remembered,' he insisted, looking at her frankly. 'He was a great benefactor of mankind, and greatly loved in his lifetime.'

'The first attribute is true, the second definitely not. From all I've picked up about Sir Lancelot, while I've been a student and a doctor here, he treated the entire St Swithin's staff like God with a hangover.'

'Why not? If it got results? It always did. And his patients all adored him,' he added, jabbing a finger.

'I accept all that,' she said graciously. 'But I'm sure you'll appreciate that in the anaesthetics department, in particular, he is a legend like a scrubbed-up Jack the Ripper.'

'I do not intend to sit here listening to a succession of family insults.'

'You know perfectly well that I should never be rude enough to insult anyone's family,' she told him bluntly. 'I have the highest opinion of your family, Hugo. I've even read some of your father's poetry.'

'Go on?' he exclaimed in amazement. 'What did you think of it?'

'Interesting. Have you anything in mind more economical than a statue?'

'As a matter of fact, I have. It is sound surgical practice to keep alternative treatment ready in case the obvious one falls flat.' He passed her a large sheet of paper with a black-and-white drawing.

'It looks like a bit of Stonehenge.'

'It's a memorial arch. The sculptor said the top bit could be removed if it became dangerous.'

'You can't leave a pile like this in the middle of the hospital courtyard. People would start complaining that the demolition lorry hadn't arrived.'

'It would be made of granite, like Aberdeen.'

'I think it should remain unquarried,' she said firmly.

'Perhaps the London pigeons might find it too convenient,' he said doubtfully, inspecting the picture.

'Why don't you simply behead your statue and use a bust?'

'That's hardly less expensive. Sculptors throw their energy into the face, you know, and regard the rest as something to prop it up. Look, I'm getting tired of this Dutch auction of Sir Lancelot's memory,' he told her severely. 'This is my final offer.' He passed her another drawing. 'How about it? A plain slab, chiselled.'

She read:

Sir Lancelot Spratt, 1890–1970
Major RAMC 1914–1918
Surgeon to St Swithin's Hospital 1925–1955
'Death is the cure of all diseases.'

'Sir Thomas Browne, *Religio Medici*,' he supplied.

'I know. A bit gloomy, isn't it?' She passed it back.

'Sir Thomas was a gloomy sod. Physicians like him are never as cheerful as surgeons. Shoving drugs into people isn't nearly as invigorating as cutting them up. It's the only solemn quote I could remember, offhand. Perhaps a Sir Lancelot quotation – "Most of my failures went up in smoke, generally at Golders Green" – would be more chipper, if they haven't now closed the crematorium.'

'Why not: "What's the bleeding time?" It's the only thing the students know that he ever said.'

'He was a bit of a slasher. To him, "keyhole surgery" was a derogatory term.'

'Now it's all the rage.'

'He would have been good at it. He tied his own fishing-flies.' Hugo smiled, looking at the ceiling. 'In his study in the country, he had a buttercup-yellow and poppy-pink sampler, stitched with: "A surgeon needs the eye of a hawk, the heart of a lion, and the hand of a lady".'

'How pretty.'

He reflected that a surgeon now needed the eye of an endo-scope, the flinty heart of an accountant, and the sleight of hand of a lawyer.

'If you still object to the monumental cost, I'll have it done in concrete like a parking impediment.'

'You'd still not have my support.'

'Well, we'll simply rename a surgical ward after him,' said Hugo, glaring as he gathered the drawings. 'That'll cost half a tin of paint.'

'You've overlooked all the signposts that will have to be altered. Hospitals are even more confusing places than airports. I assure you, I feel as generous towards a memorial for your renowned grandfather as anyone at St Swithin's, but I could never support it.'

'Why?' he demanded irritably.

'Because Sir Lancelot was an obscene anti-feminist.'

'Obscene?' Hugo stared at her. 'He had a powerful charm with women. Duchesses and film stars cheerfully let him remove all sorts of things from their insides.'

'Surely you know that Sir Lancelot made certain that St Swithin's had neither female doctors nor female students, until forced by law under the National Health Service in 1948? It's in black-and-white in the minutes of the hospital committee. You can look them up yourself, they're in the library.'

'You're like all these pressure groups, you spend all day trying to live up to your acronym,' Hugo grumbled.

'I'd rejoice for WHAMS to vanish, the morning that sexual harassment does.'

'Sexual harassment! It's normal biology. How do you suppose the human race would survive, if females weren't harassed into it?'

'That is too contemptible for comment.'

'Does it matter a damn if Sir Lancelot was an anti-feminist or a satyr, when we're gratefully erecting a monument to his lifelong and highly skilled humanitarian work?' Hugo asked angrily.

'It matters to me.'

'You *are* a silly bitch.'

'What have we got on tomorrow morning's operating list?'

'A pancreatectomy, a gall-bladder possibly, an appendix and four hernias, which the SR and the SHO can do.'

'Both female.'

'I'll have any number of females assisting me, so long as they're competent.'

Amanda rose. 'I've got a Caesar to do for Sir Edward's SR in Obs. Goodbye, darling. Do ask me for a glass of champagne at the unveiling ceremony, won't you? I'm sure I'd have absolutely loved a man like Sir Lancelot, if ever he'd have let me near him.'

Shortly after Amanda left him, Hugo slipped a dozen designs of statues, memorials and decorative doorways into his briefcase and followed her, locking the door. Would Sir Lancelot have locked the door of his office? he wondered regretfully. No one living in that age would have stolen from a hospital. But the NHS now lost millions a year from patients, visitors and unimpeded trespassers who stole by the hundreds, sheets, towels, loo paper, nappies, food, drugs, TV sets, computers, instruments, ECG machines, anything reasonably movable. They cruelly took even the cash left distractedly unguarded by the sick. Like the intruders into churches who stole lecterns, chalices, candlesticks, altar rails, Bibles, pulpits and any unattended Sunday collections. 'Conscience cloth make cowards of us all,' Hugo recalled from the script he was busily learning. But not if there was a handy market, or they had run out of the inviting articles at home.

Entering the hospital courtyard, Hugo reflected that Sir Lancelot would not have possessed an office. He would have been insulted by the suggestion. Surgeons had their wards and theatres, and offices were for clerks and such unseen persons. *Babus* and *box-wallahs*, Sir Lancelot's younger brother in the Indian Medical Service would have called them. The dean certainly had a poky, dark, freezing, dusty office beside the main gate, with one serviceable chair and a skeleton in the corner, but that was only to put aspiring medical students swiftly in their place.

The court was a wide area between the three main blocks of wards, containing four sickly trees, a pond with overfed gold-fish, and the two statues of St Swithin's doctors whose famed abilities had not saved their pursuing their patients to eter-nity. There were wooden benches for relatives to console patients if the weather was fine, waste-bins, blowing waste and pigeons. The court was far busier with doctors and their multiform helpers, and with patients in wheelchairs and on trolleys, or patients strolling, hobbling on crutches, or plonking Zimmers, or dead in a special wheeled container, than the thoughtful courts and quads of the Oxbridge colleges which Hugo had suggested as comparable ministerial victims.

St Swithin's itself had been rebuilt frequently since Richard the Lion Heart laid the now worn-hollow foundation-stone in the nave of the hospital chapel beside the great gate. It had become a jumble of buildings created from George I to George VI, and it had, like most of the City of London, been attended by the Luftwaffe demolition squads. It was rebuilt in peacetime to resemble the brand new towering blocks of flats later discovered to induce widespread psychopathy in the popula-tion, and necessitating blowing up themselves. But the hospital courtyard was much the same since it blew the zesty zephyrs of youth round the ears of the student Sir Lancelot, in the days of the glorious Empire upon which the sun never set until the blackout of World War Two.

Sir Lancelot had left no memoirs, being too busy with the scalpel for the pen. But Hugo had bundles of notes, written with surgical incisiveness, depicting St Swithin's in those innocent days when medicine and money had no connection, like those of Hippocrates, teaching and curing beneath his oriental plane tree on the island of Cos. Sir Lancelot never bothered how, or if, the hospital was financed or adminis- tered. Management was left to the Clerk of the Governors, who, from a dog-eared photograph, seemed a wing-collared gentleman of such overwhelming dignity that no one dared, or needed, to ask what he did. The Clerk's single colleague appeared to be the Lady Almoner, with an oak-panelled office by the hospital gate, where she bountifully distributed half- crowns, even ten bob notes, to the sick poor. How convenient for everybody, Hugo reflected, eyeing the site for his snubbed memorial, between the two more extravagantly venerated practitioners and the ever-flowing hospital fountain, with its goldfish.

'Ah! Hugo! I hear you're raising some sort of relic for Sir Lancelot Spratt. Would you put me down for a subscription? If somewhat modest, I'm afraid.'

'I don't care how modest, Bertie. All I want at this moment is support. The idea seems to generate all the enthusiasm of a statue to Dr Crippen.'

'He was not a St Swithin's man, I'm proud to say. But it's the natural thing; all hospitals are decorated with statues of their founders and clinical forefathers. Look at Thomas Guy, who made a fortune from the South Sea Bubble while everyone else went bust. Lister, Fleming, John Hunter in Leicester Square of all places; Liston, who could amputate a leg in two-and-a-half minutes, which I bet you couldn't—'

'I've never tried.'

'Percival Pott with his fracture, even Dupuytren with his funny fingers, in Paris somewhere I expect, all advertised by their hospitals. Look at Radcliffe, who left the best bits of Oxford.'

Bertram Whapshott was the Placenta Professor of Genetics at St Swithin's, lavishly endowed by the worldwide drug company. He wore an open white coat with a spotted red bow-tie, a bright yellow waistcoat with mother-of-pearl buttons, black-and-white check trousers and American furry boots. He was short and plump, with an eternally mobile pale face, spiky sandy hair, and protruding eyes which seemed always focused on some infinite but enchanting objective – appropriate for his specialty, Hugo always thought.

'Radcliffe made one of the shrewdest remarks in medicine.' Bertie Whapshott's mouth pouted in recollection. 'What was it? Ah— "As a young practitioner he possessed twenty remedies for every disease, and at the close of his career he found twenty diseases for which he had not one remedy".'

'Could you write that down?' urged Hugo. 'I want some sort of quote chiselled on the memorial. I don't think we'll be able to afford anything better than a slightly cheerful tombstone.'

'Oh, the observation will shortly be an out of date,' the professor assured him. 'In the past twenty years, the cures have rolled prolifically from the pharmaceutical industry – antihypertensives, anti-arrhythmics, anti-emetics, antidepressants and anticonvulsants, steroids against arthritis, bronchodilators, diuretics, healers of stomach and duodenal ulcers,' he expanded, hands in trouser pockets. 'Endocrine regulators and replacements, drugs against Parkinsonism, cytotoxic drugs against cancer. . . .'

' "Now thrive the medical armourers",' Hugo nodded, conveniently remembering a line from a previous production. The Medical School Dramatic Society favoured Shakespeare, particularly as there were no royalties to stump up.

'But haven't the diseases multiplied to match?' Hugo objected. 'Like AIDS and Alzheimer's – admittedly, he died eighty years ago – and Creutzfeldt-Jakob and. . . ?' He searched his mind. 'Well, myalgic encephalitis and repetitive strain syndrome from working computers, and post-traumatic stress, and stress from absolutely everything.'

The professor gave a laugh. 'Which are very profitable to the happy sufferers. The killing diseases will disappear. We geneticists will see to it.' His eyes rolled speculatively upwards. 'Already, we can eliminate inherited diseases like cystic fibrosis and haemophilia. Soon we shall remove the propensity for anything unpleasant. It's just a matter of jiggling the genes. Surgery will become a weird practice of the past, like blood-letting. People will still break their bones, of course, and you surgeons will be reduced to carpentry. You haven't seen my lab, I believe?'

While talking, they had been strolling across the sunny hospital square, and Hugo found himself at the door of the modern Paracelsus building. The professor swept him in. The genetics lab filled the spacious ground floor, and struck Hugo as resembling any other lab, banked with twinkling screens and filled with young people in white coats looking down microscopes.

'This is Sally.' The professor introduced a pretty, dark-haired girl. 'She does our cloning. What have you cloned today, Sally?'

She looked up from the eyepiece with a broad smile. 'A camel.'

'Carry on cloning!' smiled the professor. 'Those ancient films were wonderful, you must agree? Our envied British humour depends on two things – making the serious ludicrous, like Gilbert and Sullivan, or making the ludicrous serious, like . . . well, *Alice in Wonderland, Three Men in a Boat.* I'm sure a great poet like your father would agree?'

'Great poets haven't a sense of humour.'

Professor Whapshott prided himself on his literary indulgences, unexpected in a highly technical scientist. 'Camels are no problem,' he continued, as they moved along the lab. 'Nobody really objects to your cloning camels or sheep or cows or polar bears or giraffes or elephants; they become excited only about cloning humans. I could clone a human any afternoon I wanted.' He eyed Hugo with an eagerness approaching wildness. 'Yes! But there's a lot of fright among the political people. It's hardly a new idea. Aldous

Huxley wrote a novel called *Brave New World* in 1932, about repopulating the world with identical babies grown in bottles.'

'What will happen to all this when the hospital closes?' asked Hugo, indicating the lab.

'That is a matter of supreme indifference to me. Placenta Pharmaceuticals funds us adequately, indeed generously. Sometimes I don't know what to do with the money,' he confessed proudly. `

'But you'll have to shift, when they turn St Swithin's into a multistorey car park, or whatever.'

'Placenta has interests worldwide. We can continue our work in Milan, or Miami, or Melbourne or Montreal, or even Moscow,' he assured Hugo sweepingly.

They had reached the door with the professor's name. His office inside was large, bright, and fashionably furnished, with a bank of TV screens along one wall, so that he could see all that was going on without the bother of shifting.

'I'm sure you'd like to see my pets,' invited the professor, opening an inner door to a smaller air-conditioned room. Round its walls were cages of scurrying or sleeping guinea-pigs and rats and white mice. In the middle stood a high, oblong metal-topped table with restricting straps, somewhat chilling for animal lovers. A young bespectacled Chinaman in a white coat smiled and bowed.

'I must show you my *special* pets,' the professor exclaimed, twiddling his forefingers in his sandy hair.

Beside a window stood two densely meshed cages the size

of a TV set. As Hugo approached, a subdued buzz came from inside.

'Mosquitoes!' said the professor proudly. 'Rather remarkable mosquitoes.'

'But they're huge!'

'Oh, I could have got them as big as cock robins, had I wanted. A three-inch wingspan makes them amazingly airborne.'

'What's special about them?'

'They contain all the genes necessary to create a human being,' the professor revealed proudly, clasping a cage to him closely. 'One of these mosquitoes, of either sex, mating with a human female would make her pregnant. The human females would then, after nine months, produce identical humans. Buzzing about the place, my mosquitoes could produce such identical humans in large numbers. Though, of course, for a mosquito to enjoy sexual relations with a human female would be difficult,' he admitted. 'Even if it was a male mosquito.'

'What do they produce mating with each other?' asked Hugo, bemused.

'Mosquitoes,' said the professor with clear regret.

'Have you named the species anything?'

'Adams and Eves, of course.'

'It looks very interesting.'

The professor chuckled and slapped the cages fondly. Hugo charitably supposed that every man must be allowed his hobby.

'Now I must rudely eject you, dear boy. I have an appointment to be interviewed by a lady of the Press.'

'That sounds rather flattering. Which Press?' Hugo asked with interest.

'*Sunday Morning*!'

Hugo jumped. '*Sunday Morning*!'

'I admit its editor's phone call was a frightening interruption for a most respectable person like myself. My reaction was that they had *found out about it*. You know. We all have a guilty secret, don't we? Some of us enough for a bulky secret dossier.' The professor laughed. 'Which *Sunday Morning* would feel devilishly dutiful to expose. I agree, that newspaper is a hellish laundry for the nation's dirty washing. The vivid, tattered garments, ripped from the backs of august citizens, flap on its clothes-lines each Sunday in the shadowless sunshine of shame and the brisk breezes of national merriment,' he concluded grandly.

'Indeed,' said Hugo.

'But *Sunday Morning* had to my relief not yet *found out about it*. It is inviting me to provide a profile for Paula Smith.'

'Oh, I've often read her. She's very good. Some of her profiles are insulting, some are fair. Perhaps all are both? I wish you luck. Now I must go. I've got a private patient.'

'Ah! Not to be kept waiting.'

Hugo left for the Nightingale building, which was beyond the Paracelsus one. Its ground floor housed the consulting-rooms for the St Swithin's private patients. As these patients were charged a fee simply for using them, the rooms contained, besides a desk and an examination couch, a petunia and a couple of pictures.

He collected his new patient's notes from the private secretary, whom he shared with two other surgeons, sat at the desk and opened the folder. She was a Ms Marigold Peacock, of Chiddingford Hall, Kent, aged twenty-five. Her GP's letter was, as usual, brief, uninformative and illegible. The door opened as the secretary admitted her. Hugo jumped to his feet, staring. He had seen a ghost.

2

WHILE HUGO SPRATT was gazing open-mouthed at his mildly alarmed private patient, Paula Smith was paying off her taxi at the main entrance of St Swithin's.

She stood for a moment observing the tall, stout railings stretching along the street, on which tearjerking posters implored everyone to *Save St Swithin's*. To this purpose, grateful former patients were menacingly rattling collecting-tins on the pavement. She entered the hospital's great gate, which was erected in the eighteenth century and depicted in stone a Herculean Hippocrates with a lavish complement of traditional snakes and winged staffs. It surprised her that Londoners were pouring through it in both directions. She had not learnt that hospitals, like railway stations, are uncomfortably crammed with humanity, those there in the hope of curing outnumbering those hoping to be cured.

Paula Smith addressed the porter, uniformed in frock-coated blue-and-purple St Swithin's livery, within a lodge littered with curling notices.

'I'm looking for Professor Whapshott.'

He seemed nonplussed.

'Professor Whapshott,' she repeated. 'I've an appointment.'

He scratched his nose.

'Is he medical or surgical?'

Paula shrugged, being uninstructed in such technology. 'I wouldn't know.'

'Can't say we've got a Professor Whapshott. What's he professor of?'

'Genetics.'

'Genetics?' The porter still looked lost. 'You a patient?'

'Of course I'm not. I've come to interview him. He's the most important man in the world.'

'Go on?'

'I'm from *Sunday Morning*.'

'Are you, now?' The porter looked more interested, smirked and reached for a battered hospital phone book. Paula was aware of anxious humans gathering pushfully at the lodge window behind her.

'Why, you're quite right,' the porter exclaimed. 'Professor Whapshott, genetic lab. We don't get much call for the genetics, everyone wants out-patients, the delivery suites, or accident and emergency.'

'And how do I get there, please?'

'It's the Paracelsus building,' he indicated. 'Quickest way is across the courtyard, through a narrow archway between physiotherapy and the mortuary, take the alley by psychiatry and you'll see it past the porters' cafeteria opposite the furniture store. Can't miss it. Though I can ring through, if you like,' he offered.

'I'll find it. There seem a lot of other lost people waiting to talk to you.'

The gate led into the hospital courtyard, where she picked her way through the clinical traffic. Paula Smith was small, slight, fair, ordinary-looking, wearing a neat grey suit that merited her meeting the greatest man in the world, her age eternally thirty.

She was lost.

An archway between *what* and the mortuary? A pale, dark young man and a blonde young woman were approaching in white coats, stethoscopes collaring their necks, flanking a tall, greying, handsome man in a smart suit.

'I'm looking for Professor Whapshott.'

The trio continued talking busily.

'*Excuse me!* I'm after Professor Whapshott.'

They walked on.

'Hey! You three. Can't you help someone who's hopelessly lost in your own hospital?'

They stared at her in astonishment.

'You want something?' the senior man asked distantly.

'Professor Whapshott, if it's not too much to ask.'

A doctor is by upbringing conditioned to helping his fellow humans, whatever their predicament. 'You mean the genetic Whapshott?' he asked. Paula nodded encouragingly. 'Where's he hang out?' he asked the others. 'Wouldn't he co-habit with the anatomists?'

'He's between the porters' cafeteria and the furniture store,' Paula helped them.

'I wouldn't know about places like that,' he assured her solemnly.

'Don't you remember, sir?' asked the young man. 'He moved into that new lab in the Paracelsus, when some drug company suddenly showered him with tons of money.'

'Whapshott, of course! Our paths do not much entwine,' the tall one satisfactorily explained the situation.

'It's somewhere down there.' The woman in the white coat pointed. 'Go past accident and emergency, you can't miss it, there'll be lots of patients waiting about on trolleys.'

'How's the urine?' The tall man resumed their conversation and walk.

'Normal,' said the young man.

'Really? Better do an IVU, I suppose. What happened to that sticky hysterectomy?'

'The path report says no MRSA.'

'Good!'

They marched away, in the preoccupying, everlasting, if generally unvictorious, but always unquestioned, campaign on varied fronts to preserve human life until it surrendered to bumbling senility. The well-tailored consultant was Sir Clarence Strangewood, one of the few St Swithin's knights since Sir Lancelot. He had captured the elusive, over-hunted 'K' at a younger age than the deceased surgeon, but he was a gynaecologist who had the low-down on the lower end in the highest places.

Paula Smith reached the Paracelsus building through an area of the hospital that seemed in its desolation and disrepair to anticipate its proclaimed closure. She asked a young man in a white coat for Professor Whapshott, following him down the lab while eyeing its activities with professional closeness. Her views on science were of poetical vagueness. She realized that there were causes for leaves falling in the autumn, the sunset, the tides, sour milk, earthquakes, refrigerators, electric light, the movements of the stars and planets, and life and death, but her mind was too busy to ponder upon them.

Her impression of a laboratory was more definite, from films and advertisements, a glittering arcade of microscopes, bubbling glassware and vaporizing vivid test-tubes, peopled by earnest persons in spotless stiff white coats. The image seemed to fit. She wondered what they were all doing.

Since becoming a pushy reporter on her local newspaper at the age of seventeen, Paula had interviewed items of humanity as varied as a doctor's patients. But professors were unknown to her. She had misgivings about her ability expertly to reduce them to the customary malleability of her victims. Or she might be confronted with a Mad Prof, with wild eye and leering mouth and twitching fingers, avid to perform devastating experiments in the weirdly flickering light of his burning beliefs, and scaring her out of her poised literary style.

'Paula Smith! How do you do! What a delight to meet you.' Bertie Whapshott in his white coat rose from his office chair and clasped her hand. 'I'm a great fan of yours, a great fan. Read you every Sunday. Would you like some coffee? Though

I expect, being a journalist, you'd prefer whisky or brandy or vodka or something like that?'

'Coffee would do perfectly.'

He ordered into a desk microphone: 'Janet, two coffees and chokkie bikkies.'

Professor Whapshott seemed as harmless as the man behind the counter in her local chemist's.

'You're aware that this splendid hospital is threatened with extinction?' he reminded her. 'A cause which your newspaper has taken to its stridently righteous heart,' he added in a congratulatory tone. 'For a century, you know, *Sunday Morning* was produced in Fleet Street, barely an ambulance ride away from us. That's before all the newspapers disappeared down the Thames towards Southend-on-Sea. In those days, the staff, from editor to copyboy, regularly presented to St Swithin's their injuries and illnesses, many of which were of alcoholic origin.'

He laughed.

'You don't mind this?'

Sitting beside him, she placed a tape-recorder on the desk.

He leant forward and whispered conspiratorially: 'Haven't you got one in your bra?'

'Not when I put it on this morning.'

'For recording guilty conversations. You must tell me all the sexual secrets of famous persons.'

'I think you'd find them extremely boring.'

A young secretary brought the coffee.

'Why?'

'Because you're the most important man in the world.'

'Really? Am I? For what reason?' he asked, looking surprised but pleased.

'I interviewed the man who runs Gigantic TV last week, and he told me you were.'

'Oh, old Dickie.' The professor smiled widely. 'Sugar?'

'No, thank you.'

'Dickie had a great talent for exaggeration, you know, even before he could put it to such profitable use in his political programmes. We were schoolboys together.' He mentioned one of England's flintily enduring public schools. 'Dickie was famous as a dreadful liar. He addressed the last old school dinner, which I went to for some reason. He seems peculiarly fond of the ancient place. I suppose he feels nostalgia for his abandoned homeland of respectability before he descended into television. He made a terribly good speech, stinking with scandal. I simply sat next to him, and told him of the work I do here. It seemed to fire his imagination. I suppose that's his job? He wanted to sign me up for a series called *Unzip Your Genes*, or some such, but I declined.'

'He said you'd be perfectly happy to be interviewed.'

'I'm really a very modest man. And I'm always careful what I say.' He looked suspiciously at the tape-recorder. 'But these days – unlike such fellow research workers as Pasteur, or Marie Curie of the radium, or Roentgen of the X-rays – one must be sensitive towards public relations.'

'Well, perhaps we can make you as famous as them,' Paula suggested in a workmanlike way. 'What exactly do you do?'

She opened a notebook.

'Genetic experiments,' he instructed her, folding hands on yellow waistcoat. 'Though genetics are as misplaced in a hospital as spirituality in a bank. Hospitals are curative institutions, not preventive ones. It's in their bricks and mortar. Many were founded when the only disease you could prevent was smallpox, using Dr Jenner's eighteenth-century vaccination. Some other diseases got better naturally, despite the most dreadfully uncomfortable treatment they inflicted on the patients. Everybody else died in the wards. Supposing I could prevent all disease occurring, through genetic manipulations, next week? Why, I should throw the entire medical staff of St Swithin's out of work. Hardly make me popular.'

'But *could* you?' she asked shortly.

'Yes,' he said, looking immensely self-satisfied.

Paula made a note.

'I spent all yesterday researching you,' she revealed. 'But all I know about DNA is that it's convenient for identifying rapists.'

'Surely you've heard about Crick and Watson? Two bright boys who discovered the double helix in Cambridge after the last war?'

She nodded. 'Genes – I think of them as little fires burning on branches inside us.'

'How very poetic.'

Professor Whapshott took from his desk a thin paperback.

'Read this. *Genetics for Medical Students*. By me. If medical students can understand it, a woman of your intelligence certainly can. I lecture the students here once a week, though the attendance is most discouraging. They are much more interested in the spectacular slashings of surgery.'

The professor suddenly looked woebegone.

'At clinical meetings, nobody took much notice of me for years,' he divulged pathetically. 'Other professors were provided lavishly with assistants, to give them time to think. They had complicated apparatus by the roomful, which bolstered the ego, if not advancing the research. I had only a man to look after the mice. I'd no space, though admittedly Fleming discovered penicillin in a tiny lab, all alone. Indeed, he wasn't there at all. He was on holiday in Scotland when the *penicillium* mould grew, and ate up some staphylococci germs he'd carelessly forgotten to disinfect. It's an intriguing story.'

'I'm sure.'

'Then, suddenly—' His eyes rolled, his face lit. 'Placenta Pharmaceuticals saw the value of my work. Now I have everything I want.' He threw aside his arms. 'Have another chokkie bikkie?'

'No, thank you.'

'When you're presented with fat sums of academic money, to spend it all is surely not a temptation but a duty?'

She agreed.

'But what do you do, day by day?' she asked, looking mystified. 'Cloning?'

He waved cloning aside. 'That's as simple as using a photo-copier. You take an unfertilized egg, remove the controlling nucleus and the mitrochondria—'

'What's a mitrochondria?' she asked, writing.

'Small bodies in the cytoplasm concerned with cell respiration. Cells have to breathe, you know, like us huge walking collections of them.' He laughed. 'Then you take another cell from an adult human or animal – sheep, elephant, giraffe, hippo, or whatever you're wanting to reproduce – remove its nucleus, and insert it into the unfertilized egg. You pop that into a surrogate mother and wait.'

'For a baby hippo?'

'Or whatever. Of course, cloning renders unnecessary all the fun and games of copulation, which people might object to. But I really can't understand the fuss about cloning humans. There are so many of us, what can a few clones matter? It's those committees, mostly composed of newly ennobled scientists. Did you realize that the House of Lords is the keeper of the nation's genes?'

'Perhaps we should turn it from a hereditary House to a cloned House?'

The professor suddenly leant forward, mouth working, eyes bulging.

'I'll tell you exactly what I do, my life's work. But until it's perfected, I don't want it published.'

She nodded. 'Off the record.'

'I create perfect human beings, who live for ever.'

'Go on?' she responded calmly.

He turned to the microphone. 'Jiang, bring a specimen of Adam and Eve.'

The Chinaman appeared wearing surgical gloves, leaving a

small cage closely imprisoning two buzzing insects.

'But those mosquitoes are huge!'

'Size is the least of their unique qualities,' the professor told her proudly. 'The mosquitoes contain carefully modified genes. They would create a man, or a woman, free from suffering any known disease. Surely it's common knowledge, that we can prevent certain diseases, even the propensity for certain diseases, being transmitted from generation to generation?'

'Yes, *Sunday Morning* ran a series on it.'

He thrust his face closer. 'In my research, I found that our susceptibility to certain apparently unrelated diseases was linked. Then I found that the *links* were linked. You follow? Then I discovered a single group of molecules that controlled *all* the links. I had found the cause of our becoming ill with *anything*. The cause of our becoming aged. The cause of our going mad. We were never intended to fall to bits, to wither away, to rave, to suffer infections, pain, death itself, when we were created in the Garden of Eden by God – if you believe all that rubbish. This experiment I have been conducting since I first felt the intense attraction of genetics, and made it my life's work. When I finish it, I shall win the Nobel Prize,' he informed her.

'I shall watch out for it.'

'The only difficulty remaining is giving these perfect genes a human shape,' he confessed irritably.

'Can't the mosquitoes do it themselves?'

He shook his head sadly.

'They seem very fond of each other.'

'Yes, they are copulating. Living usually in separate cages, I expect they rather look forward to it. Eve will lay her fertilized eggs in a little water, which we supply. Very little – in nature, a rain-filled hoof-print, an empty can of beans will do. A couple of days, and the eggs become wriggling larvae. She will lay two or three hundred of them. It all makes mosquito control in the tropics so difficult.'

'The eggs will turn into three hundred little mosquitoes – instead of your dream of three hundred little humans who can eat, drink and be merry, but tomorrow never die?'

'Exactly. Transferring to a human so complex a combination of genes – as I have created – would have serious technical difficulties, which I am at the moment keenly addressing. The cloning technique offers the best solution, were it not for human stupidity and terror of scientific advances.'

'Surely,' Paula suggested helpfully, 'if you did this cloning thing, and paid the surrogate mother a lot of money, she'd keep her mouth shut? And I mean a proper lot. We'd give her a million for the story, if we heard about it.'

'The story would come out, of course,' he said gloomily. 'If I found how to produce a perfect baby from a womb situated in some remote spot like Chad or Zaire, the world would soon shake with horror. So would the House of Lords. I should be sent to jail. Or hanged from the St Swithin's great gate.'

She wrote in her notebook: *Obviously mad*.

'Right. Can I have another chat when I've checked my copy,

Professor? I must get these erudite facts right. And bring a photographer?'

'Tonight I leave on a lecture tour in America,' he announced impressively. 'Harvard, Yale, the Johns Hopkins, the University of California at Los Angeles, and so on. Then I am consulting with Placenta headquarters in Yokohama. To the Japanese, I owe the enthusiastic understanding of my work, an enthusiasm which provided its abundant facilities. They seem to have the right mentality. They seek perfection in everything. I'll be back on Thursday week. Shall we resume then? Nothing new will have happened, I assure you. Genetics is a leisurely science.'

'Can I ask you out to lunch?'

'How kind of you. *The Times* took me to Simpson's in the Strand, the *Observer* to the Savoy, the *Telegraph* to Claridge's, and I should like to try the theatrical Ivy.'

'Can I take the mosquitoes? I'll bring them back.'

'No!' He clasped his hands round the cage, in which the love-making had finished. 'You might as well ask King Arthur for a loan of the Holy Grail.'

'I'll book the Ivy for Friday week,' she settled.

3

HUGO COLLECTED HIMSELF. 'Please sit down.'
He indicated the patients' chair. The patient herself
seemed to imagine that the doctor had leapt up from polite-
ness. After all, she was a paying one.

'Well, now. It's Marigold Peacock—'

'My mother was entranced with a display of marigolds
outside the private hospital window, when she gave birth.'

'Indeed?'

'Aren't I fortunate they weren't tulips or hyacinths or
buttercups?'

'Indeed, yes. And you're twenty-five. Occupation?'

'I'm between jobs and between marriages. Though I'm
concentrating on getting another job before another husband.
Marriage brings a useful shake-up of the priorities, I found.'

'Indeed, indeed!'

He stared at her, deeply uneasy. At second glance the
resemblance was even more striking. It was frightening,
unnatural. If she wasn't a ghost – and she seemed solid
enough, in her lime silk shirt and well-cut black trousers, with
her shoulder-strap Gucci handbag – then she had conscien-

tiously perpetuated a face across a century. Unbelievable! Perhaps he should have a word with Professor Whapshott?

'And what job?'

'I'm a historian.'

He felt impelled to find more about her. 'Which university, may I ask?'

'Cambridge.'

'So was I,' he responded chattily. 'My college was Selwyn.'

'I was at Trinity. I was spoiled, I had delicious rooms on Great Court.'

'Good degree?' he asked amiably.

'I managed a first, so I went mad and I got another in business studies at Philadelphia.'

Hugo was impressed.

'I was one of those irritating prodigies, you know,' she apologized. 'I won my scholarships at sixteen, then nobody knew what to do with me. I had to kick my heels, but in extremely unexciting places. Such a pity that nobody grasps the possibilities, and the stark realities, of leisure or of marriage, before plunging into either.'

'Indeed, absolutely.'

'You are saying "indeed" rather a lot.'

'Am I? Oh, sorry.'

Odd, he thought, other patients never dared any back-chat.

'I've just been working at the Social Services Research Centre. Boring on the surface, fascinating when you burrow. But I got tired of the people in charge, who were dim-witted, obstructive and officious.'

'I know Chiddingford Hall, in Kent—'

'A temporary address. I'm lodging with my parents until I reorganize my domestic arrangements. Marriage I discovered to be largely a domestic arrangement, you can have sex with anyone you like. My ex-husband having neither money, nor sensitivity, nor brains – isn't it funny, you never speak harsher of anyone except those you deeply loved? – refuses to leave our flat. On Monday, I am having bailiffs evict him, and he'll have to buy a cardboard box from Harrods and sleep on Chelsea Embankment. He always liked to be fashionable.'

'Bailiffs? Indeed! Sorry!' he remembered. 'Well, any children?'

'Nor any intention thereof.'

It was difficult with a talkative patient – particularly a private patient – to skip unwanted information, even to leave it impolitely unacknowledged. Now Hugo could not get enough of it. What a strange young woman! He picked her GP's letter of referral from his desk, attempting to understand the handwriting.

'You were something of a prodigy yourself, surely? You won the glittering prizes which the surgical world offers,' she adapted, 'to those with stout hearts and sharp – scalpels, I suppose.'

She has been assessing my worth in the *Medical Directory* in the public library, he reflected. An increasingly unwelcome habit among private patients.

'I failed to get the top Lister Prize,' he said ruefully. 'It went to a female.' He must interrupt the sprightly chat, he had patients to see in the wards. 'What's the trouble?'

'A swelling on my abdomen.'

'Where?'

She pointed to her middle.

'Perhaps you'll lie on the couch and remove enough clothes for me to see it?'

A small lump under the skin, superficial to her right rectus abdominis muscle.

'I was worried, because it's my principle that any lump must be seen by a doctor.'

'Very wise,' he agreed. 'It's a lipoma. A soft tissue tumour, perfectly benign.'

'What shall I do?'

'Forget it.'

She sat up, buttoning her shirt and pulling up her trousers.

'I worried it could be a malignant melanoma, from lying in the sun.'

He shook his head. 'I'll write a letter to your GP. You needn't see her again.'

'I feel so much better.'

He smiled with self-esteem – a patient examined, informed, reassured and dressed.

'Though I feel a nuisance, causing all this elaborate routine.' She was sitting on the examination-couch.

'Every doctor's job is to make his patient better. If he can work out an effective way of doing it, nobody should complain.'

'How do I pay?'

'I'll send you a bill. The hospital will send another, for use of this rather bleak room. It's one of the minor paradoxes of the National Health Service. It assists the economy of both St Swithin's and the nation.'

'There's another thing.'

'Yes?'

'I want to be a nurse.'

'A nurse!' Again, he stared open-mouthed.

'You seem rather surprised. I realize that, however exacting the job, it will be a waste of my academic qualifications. But those are in a different corridor of my life. I am a practical woman, I have the reasonable, and widespread, idea of justifying my existence by helping the existence of others. Can you help me?'

'The nursing school here might put you into the next intake,' he said, feeling confused. 'I don't know how you'd go about it. I don't know any more about how they run the nursing school than how they run the kitchens. But they're as short of nurses as the Health Service of money. The two are connected.'

'I'd soon learn the prax.'

'The prax!' he cried. She looked startled. 'It's the word *she* used.'

'Who used?'

' "Prax", meaning the practical. She went to a religious hospital at Kaiserswerth, on the Rhine, to learn the prax, while her parents took the waters at Carlsbad.'

'I don't follow.'

'Come here.' He grabbed her wrist and pulled her off the couch. The polite unravelling of the mystery had gone far enough. 'Look at that picture.'

She stared at a large, modestly framed copy of a painting which decorated the consulting-room.

'Look!' he commanded. 'The lady in the picture. Don't you resemble her?'

'Do I?'

He handed her a mirror from his desk.

'Perhaps there is some resemblance,' she agreed, without interest.

'It's quite remarkable. You're alike as two peas. Though of course, you're much younger.'

'Who is she?'

'Florence Nightingale. After all, this is the Nightingale building,' he added lamely.

Marigold glanced again from mirror to portrait. 'Do I really look like that? It's one of life's blessings, I suppose, that you only know what you look like to others extremely vaguely.'

'But she's quite good looking, surely?' he encouraged her.

The pale oval face, the soft mouth, the deep eyes, the circular eyebrows, the dark hair parted in the middle. . . .

'You're not somehow related?'

'How do you know to whom you're related, over a century or two?'

'This resemblance is of great interest to me,' he said excitedly. 'You see, the Spratts are descended in the female line from Lord Herbert. He's the handsome gentleman in the other portrait. He died aged fifty, in 1861 – everyone said because Florence Nightingale worked him to death. He was Secretary at War during the Crimean business, and she got out there to nurse the troops in Scutari only through bullying him. She had him round her little finger, unquestionably.'

'Interesting.'

'You'll find Sidney Herbert in Pall Mall, if you want to, opposite the Athenaeum Club, our refuge of the gin-drinking intelligentsia. Also yourself, in a long dress. Go and have a look.'

'I have. The Lady with the Lamp.'

'It's the wrong lamp. Florence Nightingale stands there in the middle of the traffic with a lamp like Aladdin's. In fact, she wandered the wards with a collapsible tubular Turkish Army one, like a candle in a pink concertina.'

Marigold was unexcited with his unique discovery.

'Can I see you again?' he asked, hardly believing that he had done so.

She looked startled.

'Socially, you know. Forgive me, but . . . well, your resemblance to Florence Nightingale utterly fascinates me. You have her tremendous intelligence, too.'

'Isn't this rather irregular, a surgeon dating his patients when he's just taken their clothes off?'

'Not at all.' Hugo looked offended. 'Yes, as a matter of fact, it is,' he reflected. 'Though it isn't professional misconduct for a doctor to dine with his patients, no more than to share the hospital tea and biscuits with them.'

She smiled again. 'I won't tell on you.'

'I've a little scheme that might interest you.' It had come to his mind as he examined her abdomen. 'To help save the hospital from its threatened closure. The hospital which you might be joining shortly as a nurse,' he added slyly.

'I think you'd find me dreadfully boring, when not offering the interest of a patient.'

'Could you meet me tomorrow evening, for a drink?' he persisted. 'In the students' bar. That's in the medical school, on the far side of the hospital. They don't mind the odd consultant appearing, it amuses them to buy us drinks, like feeding the animals in the zoo. I'm often in there. There's a hall next door with a stage, where I put on shows. I'm president of the students' dramatic society.'

Her face expressed recollection. 'There was something in *Sunday Morning*. Your mother's Fran Francis. She's in loads of old films on the telly.'

'Yes, she worked a lot with Nöel Coward. He was my godfather. There were suggestions of fatherhood, but I don't think that was after his fashion.'

'And your father's Peregrine Spratt, great poet, novelist, critic and culture buff.'

'My grandfather was a surgeon here – Sir Lancelot Spratt, I'm erecting a statue to him – and he thought my father was an evolutionary mutant.'

'I shouldn't be asking you personal questions. Only you me.'

'It makes a change, sometimes.'

She was an extraordinary woman to meet unexpectedly on a sunny May Monday morning. Apart from the jolting resemblance, there was something unidentifiable but disturbing about her. From the moment she sat across the desk he felt uncomfortably that she was a woman he knew, and to whom he owed deference, instead of the conventional reverse.

'You've probably got a hundred things to do at six o'clock tomorrow evening,' he apologized quickly.

'I'm not very sociable. Unlike my sister Pamela. You're always seeing her in the gossip columns and magazines.'

'Oh, are you?'

'Unfortunately, I dislike insincerity, without which social life is unworkable. I wanted to do something useful in life. Quite reasonable, surely? My sister seeks happiness in amusements, which is more difficult, I think.'

'She must have an enviable income.'

'My father owns Peacock's Bank. You could see it from the hospital, if you climbed on the roof.'

'Peacock's Bank?' He wondered if he could touch her for a subscription to Sir Lancelot's statue. 'I hope your father approves of your own admirable choice of lifestyle?'

'Entirely. Doing something useful is the most gratifying of occupations, surely? Also the most treacherous. Many people who think they are doing so are doing exactly the opposite, and making themselves awful nuisances into the bargain.'

'Yes, it's pleasant to be important for what you do, like a – well, a surgeon or an actress – rather than for what you are, like a princess.'

'I could have worked in the family bank, but I'm not very fond of fiddling with futures and options and derivatives and so on. Your science is an infinitely better application of mathematics than the stock market.'

'Indeed, I agree. Though you must become a financial expert these days to survive as a consultant in the NHS. I'm not very good at it. I'm always losing my credit cards.'

'I'm taking a lot of your time, which your secretary outside impresses upon me as priceless.'

'On the contrary, it is a pleasure to find such an interesting patient.'

'Indeed?' She smiled. 'Now I'm saying it.'

As Marigold Peacock quit the Nightingale Building, the third woman that day of catastrophic significance to St Swithin's was entering the great gate.

Mandy Miles, impelling with stern-faced resolution a pushchair containing her firstborn, her one-year-old son Scott, had ignored in her haste the porter's lodge to explore the confusing entrails of St Swithin's.

The always frightening path for patients at St Swithin's was, like all NHS hospitals, smoothed with generous signposting. Mandy had given birth in its obstetrical department, she had dutifully attended its ante- and post-natal clinics, but the memory of this fundamental episode in her otherwise shallow but pleasant life had already faded. Like Paula, like most visitors, she was soon lost.

She turned to the middle of the hospital courtyard, where arose a tall, blue-and-white many-fingered signpost propelling people in all directions. Mandy had to choose between Pathology, Crèche, Medical Out-patients, Consultants' Car park, Haematology, Enquiries, Nutrition, . Occupational Therapy, Lecture Theatres, Cafeteria, Day Surgery, Toilets and Hospital Chaplain. Deciding sensibly that Crèche might be getting warm, she transported her baby briskly towards it across the busy flagstones.

She was rewarded with a door in the far corner marked Post-natal Mothers and Babies, with an injunction for them not to smoke. Parking the buggy outside, she carried Scott across a grubby apartment containing three long benches crowded with similar units of human reproduction to her own.

The flaking walls were largely hidden with bright posters, stridently urging patients to take advantage promptly of the prophylactic, dietetic, gymnastic, remedial, behavioural, social and financial measures conscientiously concocted for their benefit by their diverse professional guardians, all collected under the outlandishly diverse roofs of sprawling St Swithin's. She stopped against one of the numerous folder-loaded counters, guarded by one of those middle-aged women in a white overall, towards which all the tragedies and torments which dragged humanity to St Swithin's must first be addressed.

'Yais?' invited the white-overalled woman.

'I've got to see the doctor.'

'Which one?'

Mandy struggled to remember. 'He's Sir Clarence some-thing. It's important.'

The woman held out her fingers. 'Have you got your hospital card?'

'Of course I haven't got my bloody hospital card. It's not my fault I'm here at all. It's yours. You just wait,' Mandy threatened fiercely.

This impatient response was explicable by Mandy's having left home in Hackney in an anger which had ignited at Christmas, burned steadily through the winter and spring, and that Monday morning had exploded into activity. It had raged on the bus, glowed red walking from the bus stop, and turned incandescently white as she trod the flagged pavements of its cause.

'Would you mind?' invited the woman, blasé to all emotional states. 'Were you one of his patients?'

'I was, and I wish I never had been,' Mandy replied furiously. 'I've something to tell him that he isn't going to like. Not one little bit, he isn't.'

'May I ask what?' said the woman mildly.

'No, you can't. It's personal.'

'Well, you can't see Sir Clarence Strangewood if you haven't got an appointment,' the woman disposed of the situation. 'His clinic's overbooked this morning already. I can make you one for next month,' she conceded. 'Though first you'll have to bring your hospital card.'

'If you must know, *this* is the reason.'

Mandy thrust towards her a fair-haired, pink-checked child, in a bobbled blue-and-white knitted hat and a blue-and-white knitted jumper, who with admirable placidity was observing the busy hospital scene and sucking a dummy.

The woman receded behind her counter from the offered explanation.

'There's something wrong with your baby?'

'What's wrong with my baby is that he's the wrong baby.'

'How do you mean?'

'It's bloody plain, isn't it? I came here to have my baby and they gave me the wrong one to take home.'

'How do you know?' the woman asked calmly.

'Because he doesn't look a scrap like me or my husband, that's why. People are beginning to talk. I want my own baby back.'

Mandy was now shouting, gathering the baby and banging the counter with her free hand.

'Something the matter?' enquired a young woman in a blue dress and a white cap.

'She says she's been given the wrong baby, Sister.'

'It just can't happen.' The out-patients' nursing supervisor dismissed the fuss. 'You're upsetting everyone.' Sister indicated the gawping patients on the benches with their variously misbehaving infants.

'If you're worried, you'd better see the social services,' she advised. 'I expect they have lots of these sort of cases. People are always complaining,' she chided. 'About absolutely everything.'

'I want to see the doctor.'

Mandy's free hand grabbed the white-coated arm of the young man with the stethoscope who had accompanied Sir

Clarence in the courtyard, and was now hurrying from the clinic entrance towards its inner door.

'What's up?' he asked in alarm, detaching himself forcefully.

'She says she was sent home with another patient's baby, Doctor,' said Sister.

'It's cruel. It's horrible. You've got to do something about it,' Mandy demanded, starting to cry.

'There, there,' said the young doctor absently.

He was in a period of delightful self-appreciation after passing the daunting specialist diploma in obstetrics, the MRCOG, which demanded exhaustive knowledge of its subject, if nothing about wrongfully distributed babies.

'Have a little sit down,' he prescribed. 'Sister'll get you a nice cup of tea.'

He hurried into the consulting-room, where enthroned behind the desk no patient could lay hands on him, nor dare to think of it.

A mother holding a month-old infant squeezed kindly along the crowded bench, letting Mandy flop beside her.

'What's the matter, luv?' the other mother asked kindly.

'I can't tell you.' Mandy was now feeling confused, blowing her nose on a tissue.

That moment, Sophie Kingston arrived at the desk, impatiently pushing Jeremy in his buggy.

'Yais?' greeted the white-overalled woman.

'I wish to see Sir Clarence Strangewood, please. It's about an important matter.'

'Have you got your hospital card?'

'I tore it up. I never want to see it again. I never want to see this hospital again. By the time I've finished, its reputation will anyway be absolute zero, believe you me.'

The woman behind the counter sighed. 'What's the matter? Someone send you home with the wrong baby?'

Sophie stared at her. 'How did you guess?'

The woman leant over the desk and shrieked.

The fair, pink baby in a pink knitted hat sucking its dummy in Sophie's buggy was identical to the baby sucking its dummy on the bench in Mandy's arms.

4

THESE TWO COMPLAINING mothers were unacquainted.

Mandy was twenty-six, and wore jeans and an old T-shirt imploring SAVE THE WORLD. When she was twenty, she had urged SAVE THE WHALES. She was vague what the whales should be saved from, or for, and imagined them as playfully squirting seagoing elephants, but the righteous message provided a mild feeling of self-importance otherwise lacking from her stereotyped existence. She had been advised in the pub that whales were now out-of-date, but no substitute for salvation presented itself except the trees, which from observation did not seem to need it. She discarded minatory tops until someone in another pub, terrified at the vanishing ozone layer, sold her the one she had on, which was conveniently comprehensive.

Mandy was slight, dark and pretty, she wore five rings on her fingers and one on her ears. Her husband Jim was an under-manager of a supermarket (he filled the shelves). They lived in a semi-detached house, resolutely bought by Jim's father from the council and re-fronted in Tudor style. She had been married six years, during which their diligent sexual effort had joyously produced Scott.

Sophie was twenty-nine, fair, pink and sturdy, wearing a matching Jaeger jumper and skirt. She lived in a three-storey terrace house in Islington, her husband Edwin was an accountant (among a financial regiment deployed by a City firm), and her son Jeremy was the culmination of five years' painstaking sexual endeavour. In immiscible British society, Mandy was working-class and Sophie was middle-class. It is an overlooked, but overwhelming, function of the National Health Service to outdo the politicians and unite the nation in classless anguish.

The two women had given birth at St Swithin's on the same day, Monday, 2 April, Mandy at 2.30 in the morning, Sophie at 10 a.m. Their labours were normal and they had gratefully left the hospital two afternoons later, without encountering one another in the busy obstetrical wards. The babies once home were delightedly exposed to unfeigned admiration, were fed, dosed and cleaned according to the standardized and well-advertised practices of modern motherhood. They slept with admirable depth; they were amazingly good-tempered and virtuous; they attained the harshly imposed benchmarks of early life – gurgling, crawling, toddling, teeth-sprouting – with gratifying promptitude. Their poo-poos were regular, their wee-wee was of tidal predictability. The parents of both were rightfully pleased with themselves at producing offspring of such unusual normality.

After six months, spooky shadows began to gather round the cots.

'Oh, int'ee luvley?' exclaimed Mandy's friend Linda, encountering Scott in his buggy outside Marks and Spencers. It was a chilly October Saturday morning, the child well wrapped-up in woollies, blue eyes bright, cheeks rosy, insouciantly sucking his dummy. It was the first time her friend Linda had eyed him since midsummer.

Linda hesitated, frowning. 'He don't look much like you, though, does he?' she assessed, head on one side.

The frankness of friends is impregnable, however infuriating.

'He's a boy, o'course,' Mandy dismissed the criticism. 'You mustn't expect him to take after his mum.'

'Oh, yais, o'course.' Linda was glad to agree to the excuse. 'Mind, he don't look much like Jim neither,' she found herself impelled to point out, adding the apology, 'If you don't mind my saying so.'

This remark struck Mandy with dreaded alarm.

For three months, since Scott began to pass from a lump of incontinent flesh to the semblance of an organized human being, Mandy and Jim had each begun to notice separately that he resembled neither of them. At first, they both dismissed the notion as a passing delusion, like failing to recognize an acquaintance across a pub. But their puzzlement and apprehension grew with the child. Neither felt it necessary – nor easy – to mention this strangeness to the other. On a Sunday morning in August, during their fortnight's holiday at Lanzarote, the baby had finished a week in the constant company of both. For twenty-four hours a day they could look at him and scratch their heads.

On the crammed beach, Mandy adjusted Scott's blue cotton hat against the sun, in which he sat coolly sucking his dummy. She could no longer stop herself saying, 'Funny, innit?'

'What's funny?' Jim in swimming briefs, larded with sun oil, lay on a towel reading through sunglasses his paperback of the year.

'Scott. He don't look much like either of us.'

Jim turned on his elbow. He was skinny, passably good-looking, sharp-faced with brown curly hair. 'I was waiting for you to say that, luv,' he revealed, with intense seriousness.

'You mean you noticed it?' Mandy's eyes widened under her scarlet baseball cap.

' 'Course I had.'

There was silence.

'Well . . . why?' asked Mandy helplessly.

'You ought to know, didn't you?'

'Jim!'

'Stands to reason.'

'Jim!' she cried, louder.

'Don't tell me who it was: I don't want to know,' he asserted firmly, turning on his back again.

She screamed. 'Jim!'

He looked round nervously. Nobody seemed to have noticed the rapidly rising drama. He recollected that they were all foreigners of various sorts, unblessed with English.

Mandy collected herself. 'I don't know how you can say such a thing,' she told him angrily.

'Stands to reason, don't it? We're trying to have a baby for years and years. Maybe my fault as much as yours. Then we suddenly have one.'

'But we went to those doctors,' she threw in the excuse.

'Fat lot of good they did,' he repelled it.

'Jim! How can you think that of me?'

He shrugged. The conversation seemed difficult to continue. 'Perhaps we're just seeing things,' he retreated.

'Perhaps we are,' she followed him gratefully.

He resumed the paperback.

The thought, once expressed, stayed solidly between them, as inescapably as the baby himself.

Home again, Jim speculated openly once or twice a week on Scott's paternity. Mandy with increasing asperity denied any irregularity. She was mentally lost. There *had been* no irregularity, but only she could know that. And if Jim would not believe her, what could she do about it? Hardly blame him, I suppose, she reflected miserably, being a sensible woman.

She stared at the baby constantly, as he lay contentedly sucking his dummy, unknowing that his pink plump flesh covered the bones of contention. More bewilderingly than his looking like neither parent, Scott looked like nobody else she knew. Nor had ever known, she decided, should his conception somehow have been miraculously deferred post-coitally.

After meeting Linda in the street that autumn, Mandy noticed increasingly the sly sympathy of her friends. They suggested unconvincingly and unenthusiastically that Scott would grow smoothly into the image of one or other of them. Children *do* change so, look at my Carlie, they exemplified, now she's just like her dad, when she was a toddler she was the spit and image of that woman on the telly doing the coffee commercials. Mandy afterwards sat earnestly watching television, carried away by the possibility of electronic pre-conceptional influences, but nobody on the box resembled Scott in the slightest.

At Christmas, they took Scott down to see his Nan at Herne Bay.

Neither Mandy nor her two elder brothers knew whether their mother had something useful put away or not. Their late father had worked behind the counter in a betting-shop and, as people who work behind the counters of sweet shops get sweets sticking to their fingers, the principle was reasoned by his children as extendible to money. Her father had enjoyed an esteemed shrewdness and a sharpness of character, which had profited Mandy's genes.

Jim drove in the first daylight down the M2 in the second-hand Mazda, Scott desirably asleep on his car-seat in the back, with the gift-wrapped bedroom slippers. Nan's immobile mobile home stood in the vast park of them beside the Kentish sea. It was a bleak, windy, unconvivial Christmas morning when they would have preferred to have stayed in bed playing with Scott. But it was more desirable to take

Christmas dinner with Nan amid the swirling sand and spitting waves than have her to stay sleeping on their sofa into the New Year.

Nan inspected her grandchild with rising curiosity during the morning. When Jim went off for a beer, she exposed her perplexity with privileged tactlessness.

'Well, I don't know. I think it's a proper disgrace.'

'What is, Mum?' asked Mandy innocently.

'I don't know 'oo the father is, but it's not your Jim, that's for sure.' She glared at Scott, angelically sucking his dummy in his detached car-chair in the corner.

'How can you say a thing like that, Mum?' poor Mandy responded weakly. A maternal accusation was to be taken with solemnity.

'We haven't had anything in the family like this before, and that's certain. All you children looked just like your poor late father. He'd be spinning in his grave at all this, believe you me, if he hadn't been cremated.'

'It's not true!' Mandy shook her head wildly. 'Scott's lovely. He just takes after someone up one of our family trees.'

'All we got up our family tree's a load of monkeys,' Nan said modestly. 'I always thought, before you married Jim, is my Mandy going to give up some of her old tricks, now?' She rubbed it in. 'I quite lost count of the men you used to go with.'

'You don't suppose I had sex with them all?' Mandy demanded, offended.

'Didn't you? You people now have sex like in my time we used to go to the cinema.'

'I tell you, Jim was the father, there couldn't be anyone else,' Mandy insisted. 'We wanted a baby, dinn't we? We went to all them clinics, trying to have one. I can't tell you the trouble, what with the operations and specimens. Jim never got over having to produce a specimen of his whatsit for them, still warm, too. *I didn't want no one but Jim to be the father,*' Mandy told her fiercely, if tearfully. 'If you can't see that, you've got a dirty mind.'

'Some funny things happen on Saturday nights,' Nan said philosophically, crouching to baste the turkey in the tiny oven.

The insult made a welcome excuse to quit Nan's seaside home shortly after the plum pudding.

In the New Year, Mandy and Jim stopped talking about it. There seemed no point, as nothing could be done to make Scott look any different. At the beginning of May, Mandy learned from *Sunday Morning*:

HOSPITAL MIX-UP COUPLES GET WRONG BABIES.

It was a hospital in the Midlands, where two couples were dispatched home with the other's infants. The mistake was corrected more swiftly than the misdirection of airline luggage. But it was a signal for action, of Trafalgar thrust.

Monday morning, she was off to St Swithin's.

The Kingstons became aware of nursing an alien later than the Mileses.

'Something worries me.'

Sophie brought the subject up.

'Worries you? What worries you?' asked Edwin absently.

They had finished eating their evening meal on their laps, their plates pushed aside. They had continued watching television into a sitcom of such deepening boredom it had driven them to conversation.

Their child was upstairs in his cot, impeccably asleep.

'Jeremy worries me. Have you looked at him carefully?'

'Of course I have.' Edwin was offended. He was short, gingery, square-faced, with a dry skin, a thin mouth and heavy eyebrows. 'Why shouldn't I look carefully at my own son?'

'Well, you didn't have to look particularly carefully, did you, to see that our son doesn't bear the faintest resemblance to either of us?'

He stared at her. It had not occurred to him before. You had a baby and presumably it took after the parents, as surely as your next year's tax demand was engendered by last year's income.

'No, I suppose he doesn't much,' he had to admit, after a few moments' consideration.

'If you're thinking of asking any awkward questions, you can put them out of your head,' she instructed him.

'What awkward questions?'

'Oh, don't be stupid,' she said impatiently.

'Oh, I see. No, no, I'd never think that. . . .'

He reflected again. A mother was immutable, but a father undetectable.

A tormenting arrangement. It had caused a lot of trouble in history and Shakespeare, he seemed to remember.

'Has anyone else noticed this?'

She nodded firmly. 'Yes. I went to a coffee-morning at Julia's, remember? Amelia was there. I wanted to show off Jeremy, quite naturally. Then Amelia said: "Have you got any Nordic blood, Sophie?" and I said: "What do you mean?" and she said: 'Well, ancestors in Oslo, and those sort of places. 'I said no, and Amelia said: "Don't worry if Jeremy doesn't look like you or Edwin, Sophie, children don't take after their parents any more, it's one of the changes in family life, I saw it in the papers," and Julia herself said: "Don't worry, Sophie, I'm sure being a boy he'll come to resemble Edwin as he grows up, it often happens,' though, of course, I knew what both of them meant.'

'If you went to bed with someone else, when the doctor assured you that you were infertile, it was sort of understandable,' Edwin observed mildly. 'No risk involved.'

She sat up straight. '*But I didn't!*' she screamed.

'Shhhh! You'll wake the baby.'

'How can you accuse me, just like that?'

'Well, the baby can't possibly be mine, now you mention it,' Edwin decided. He accepted the audit which his wife had presented. 'He doesn't look remotely like me. He looks rather like Nielsen at the office.'

'Nielsen? What Nielsen? I've never even met him.'

'Yes, you did. Wimbledon fortnight, the year before last. In our hospitality tent.'

'I don't think anyone's ever managed that sort of thing at Wimbledon.'

'I didn't mean like that.'

She said nothing. They stared at the television.

Edwin henceforth took no notice of the baby. For weeks, he was home from the office disregarding it like a busy father with the family's pet hamster. Sophie cleansed and fed Jeremy with instinctive maternal devotion, though her bubbling love for him had been cooled with icy anxiety. She and Edwin were now hardly speaking to each other. They watched television in silence. Their marriage was suffering, perhaps dying. She cursed herself for raising the subject. But something was undeniably *wrong*. The baby she had borne was definitely not hers.

The next weekend she read *Sunday Morning*, and on Monday was attacking St Swithin's.

'Two of the patients seem to be complaining about something,' said Sister, entering the small consulting-room where Mr O'Shea, the obstetrical registrar, had seated himself impregnably behind a pile of notes at the desk.

'Oh, God! What now? Staying wide awake during a Caesar? Love life ruined by tight introitus after episiotomy? Needle left in baby's bum? Hospital food poisoning? Iatrogenic dysparunia wrecking marriage? Psychoneurosis inflicted by rude doctors?'

'They say they've been given the wrong babies.'

'Oh, that. It's a wonder that half the mothers aren't saying they've got the wrong babies, after that bit in yesterday's paper. Did you see it?'

'They say the babies don't look like the fathers.'

'We all know about that situation, don't we?'

'Nor like the mothers.'

'Tell them to complain to the NHS ombudsman. It's his job, not mine. I've got to start the clinic. Look at the time. Look at that load of patients.' He slapped the pile of notes. 'I won't get my lunch.'

'I think you *should* see them,' Sister persisted. 'There's something peculiar about them.'

'What?'

'Both the babies are identical.'

'To some people, all babies look the same.'

'Not to me,' she told him crisply. 'And they're peculiar babies.'

'Peculiar how?'

She hesitated. 'They're a year old, yet somehow ... from the looks on their faces, from the way their eyes follow you about, they could be four or five.'

Mr O'Shea sighed deeply at such fantasy. 'You're imagining things.'

'If you don't believe me, see for yourself.'

'What are the mothers like?'

'Troublemakers. You could spot them a mile away.'

'All right, let them in,' he surrendered. 'But they mustn't take more than five minutes.'

'It's Mrs Miles and Mrs Kingston,' she selected from the gathered fruits of reproduction outside.

Mandy and Sophie carried in their babies. Scott and Jeremy

sucked their dummies and stared with interest at the doctor.

'You're right,' he muttered to Sister in surprise. 'They ought to be at school. You claim you were given the wrong babies?' he demanded of the visitors brusquely.

'That's obvious, isn't it?' said Mandy sharply.

Mr O'Shea was busy with the keyboard at his elbow.

'You'll admit that your two babies bear a striking resemblance?' he invited, staring at the computer screen as the mothers sat down.

'Of course we do!' said Sophie crossly. 'We've just discovered it, out there. It was a terrible shock.'

Mandy added forcefully, 'It was a shock to everyone. Wasn't it, Sister?'

'I thought they were twins,' Sister said defensively.

'Exactly,' said Mr O'Shea. 'You are making an extremely serious accusation against St Swithin's Hospital, that we sent you both home with the wrong babies?'

'You've got it right,' nodded Mandy.

'In that case, you must *each* have been given *one* of a pair of identical *twins*. Correct?'

The two mothers looked at each other.

'Mustn't you?' Mr O'Shea insisted irritably.

They looked at each other again. 'I suppose so,' admitted Sophie.

'Twins were last born in the St Swithin's maternity suite on Boxing Day,' he informed them, staring at the screen. 'I'm reading the delivery room day book. When did you have your own babies?'

They told him.

'Yes, here's your entry. The twins before that were delivered on the ninth of the previous August. They'd be tucked up at home more than six months by then. We don't seem to get many twins these days. Nor triplets, quads, or quins, they're rare chicks. Multiple births go to the old Whitechapel Lying-in, I suppose. Until the government close that, too. There you are,' he observed with finality.

'But why have we got identical babies?' Sophie asked.

'Did you know each other beforehand? Move in the same circles?' Mr O'Shea asked with pointed vagueness.

'Of course not!' Sophie was shocked at the social, not sexual, innuendo.

'Well, even if your babies do look alike, you must still have been sent out into the world with the same ones as you brought into it,' he concluded with satisfaction.

'Then why *are* our babies alike?' demanded Sophie.

'I don't know,' he confessed, shrugging.

'Why don't you know? You're the doctor,' Sophie pointed out.

'I still don't know.'

'Suppose two other mothers had the same-looking babies at the same time? We could still have been given the wrong ones,' Mandy persisted.

'This is becoming nonsensical,' said Mr O'Shea. 'If that had happened, you wouldn't have any cause for complaint, would you? Identical babies are interchangeable.'

'You're being cruel,' said Sophie.

'I'm being funny.'

'Next you'll be telling us to do a swap. Right. If the two babies are exactly the same, it doesn't make any bloody difference which of the two we bring up,' said Mandy.

'If you've any complaints about your treatment, the Government employ a man for you to write to,' Mr O'Shea told them briskly. 'Sister will give you his address. Please stop holding up the other patients.'

'You're trying to hide somefink,' Mandy accused him.

'We've nothing to hide. You've two lovely babies of your own which happen to look rather alike.' He settled the matter by adding, 'You mustn't believe all you read in the newspapers.'

'We're not leaving this hospital until we get satisfaction.' Mandy's voice rose. 'Are we?' she demanded of Sophie.

'I suppose not,' said Sophie, suddenly uncertain.

'We are not,' Mandy repeated fiercely. 'I may be just an ignorant mum, but I will not be buggered about.'

'Here's Sir Clarence,' said Mr O'Shea with relief, as the consultant came through the inner door with his blonde senior registrar.

Sir Clarence caught a whiff of mutiny on the patients' benches.

'What's going on?' he asked anxiously. 'Nothing the matter with these twins? Which of you is the mother?'

'They're not twins,' said Mandy. 'This one's mine and that one's hers.'

'They were delivered on the same day last April,' Mr O'Shea informed him.

'Yes, I remember,' Ms Holloway the senior registrar volunteered. 'I was on duty. Very fine babies, too,' she added encouragingly to the parents.

'They're claiming they were discharged from hospital with the wrong ones,' said Mr O'Shea.

'What?' Sir Clarence started. He, too, had seen *Sunday Morning*. He had picked it up from the bed of a private patient, who had gleefully drawn his attention to it.

'But how terrible . . . how terrible . . . that you two mothers should have the slightest suspicion . . . the slightest cause for suspicion. . . .'

His daily armour of superiority had been breached by the shock. He had a horror of any irregularity that could impale him with litigation, or even with gossip. It would affect his private practice.

'I'm sure a satisfactory explanation can be found,' he continued, restoring his familiar blandness.

'Give it to me, and I'll listen,' Mandy offered briskly.

'Such matters can't be cleared up in a moment, Mrs—?

'Miles. My friend's Mrs Kingston.'

'Thank you. I promise you a most thorough investigation. Unfortunately, I have to rush away to operate.'

He had half-a-dozen cases in the Nightingale private block, from which he did not wish to be delayed by awkward, quarrelsome NHS patients.

'But I shall instruct my two assistants here to make exhaustive enquiries on your behalf. A DNA test is of prime importance, I should say. Get Professor Whapshott to perform one,' he instructed Ms Holloway.

'He's left the hospital,' she informed him. 'He's booked on Concorde for a lecture tour of America, and won't be back until Thursday week.'

'These professors!' said Sir Clarence crossly. 'Forever swanning round the world in luxury instead of doing their job like the rest of us. It's a wonder they don't put advertisements for academic posts under "Travel Bargains". He's the only person I care to rely upon in such controversial matters,' he imparted. 'Whapshott's views on genetics are widely respected, and impressively delivered, even in the witness-box. Not that we shall come to that,' he added swiftly, in the direction of the mothers. 'You need have no case for concern, I guarantee.'

'That's not good enough,' said Mandy.

'I don't see what more I can offer,' Sir Clarence said, almost plaintive.

'It's a terrible emotional strain,' said Sophie.

'I'm sure it is. Mr O'Shea here will prescribe you some sedative. Why not come back on Friday week? Then we can all go and see Professor Whapshott, who is a world-renowned expert. I shall accompany you myself,' he conceded with grace. 'I'm sure with Professor Whapshott's help we can have everything thoroughly sorted out in no time.'

He congratulated himself in shifting the responsibility.

'Yes, on Friday week,' he made up their minds for them. 'I shall make a special point of being there, whatever woman in labour is demanding my attentions.'

Private, of course, he told himself, plenty of assistants to do the NHS ones.

'I see your GPs referred you both to the infertility clinic,' interrupted Mr O'Shea, peering at the screen. 'You were both seen there finally on June the second, the year before last.'

'Oh, my God,' muttered Sir Clarence in sudden alarm. 'Did they have IVF?'

'What's that?' demanded Mandy sharply.

'IVF is *in vitro* fertilization, by which we introduce ovum to sperm in glassware, to produce what's popularly known as a test-tube baby.'

'I dunno,' said Mandy. 'Did you?' she asked Sophie.

'Any possibility of malpractice?' Sir Clarence demanded in a whisper from his two professional colleagues.

Sir Clarence suffered from an anxiety neurosis, which is useful in bossy persons for gloomily predicting the worst, which generally occurs.

'Malpractice at St Swithin's? Perish the thought,' muttered Mr O'Shea cheerfully.

In a low voice, Sir Clarence confided, 'One husband's sperm might somehow have been divided in two, and mistakenly given to both mothers.'

'Impossible,' whispered Mr O'Shea consolingly.

'But it *might*,' Sir Clarence insisted. 'Human error creeps in everywhere. It's always crashing planes and sinking oil tankers. Our profession's bursting with it. Read the *Journal of the Medical Defence Union*.'

'The horror comic,' shivered Mr O'Shea.

'Why, these two mothers could even have had one woman's already fertilized pair of ova implanted in each of them,' Sir Clarence exclaimed.

'Unbelievable. But I suppose everybody thought the Virgin Birth was a load of balls at the time,' Mr O'Shea conceded politely.

'But it happened,' hissed Ms Holloway urgently. 'I remember, there was a case I saw in the *Lancet*. Or perhaps it was in *Sunday Morning*?'

'And if these two women had *in vitro* fertilization from a donor, and not from their husbands—' speculated Sir Clarence anxiously.

'They might both have used the same donor?' Mr O'Shea supplied.

'There was a gynaecologist in America, Sir Clarence, who gave his own sperm to all his infertile patients,' Sister broke in helpfully. 'He said it saved him a lot of trouble. He was sent to jail.'

'Yes, I read about that, too, in *Sunday Morning*,' nodded Ms Holloway. 'But they didn't need IVF,' she recalled suddenly, smiling. 'I remember something else, now. I did a lap and dye on both of them.'

'A lap and dye!' Sir Clarence cried. The only possible cause of the strange obstetrical coincidence – a bungled IVF – for which St Swithin's itself could be accused and perhaps condemned, had been thrown out of court.

'What are you all whispering about?' asked Sophie abruptly.

'What's a lap and dye?' Mandy persisted. 'Sounds like a sick greyhound.'

'A lap and dye is the suffusion of the Fallopian tubes in the female pelvis, a common investigation of infertility.'

Sir Clarence in his relief was glad to be informative.

'The dye is injected through the cervix of the uterus by way of the vagina, while the tubes are inspected through the lens of a laparoscope.'

'Our telescope of the entrails,' assisted Mr O'Shea.

'Which is inserted into the abdomen, below the umbilicus, under a brief anaesthetic. If the dye emerges from the upper ends of the tubes, against the ovaries, they contain no obstruction to the normal passage of the monthly egg to its nest of fertilization – the interior of the uterus.'

Sir Clarence demonstrated with gestures of elegant anatomy.

'There it would meet the sexual partner's sperm, which has already been tested for its potency. If obstruction of the Fallopian tubes is discovered, this can be operated upon. If none – well, we have to scratch their heads and think again.'

He gave a cultivated laugh.

'All is performed as a day-case, necessitating but an hour or so's rest afterwards, before the patient can be driven to the welcome comfort of home.'

'I remember every minute of it,' said Sophie, as Mandy nodded vigorously.

'I'm sure you do.'

'You found nothing wrong with me.'

'Nor me.'

'Oh?' said Sir Clarence, looking apologetic.

Mr O'Shea had been busily flicking the keyboard.

'At the infertility clinic, Mrs Miles was done at eight-thirty in the morning, Mrs Kingston at twelve, the same day,' he confirmed from the screen.

'And I got pregnant the very next month,' said Mandy.

'So did I,' exclaimed Sophie.

'Yours are not the first cases,' smiled Sir Clarence indulgently. 'The investigation of infertility is often its cure. Curious. I am at a loss to explain why. My psychiatric colleagues supply a ready explanation, as they do for everything. You must have met each other when you came for your operation?' he added, suddenly suspicious of a long-laid plot.

'We'd never set eyes on each other until this very morning,' Sophie assured him. 'She'd gone home from the clinic before I arrived.'

'It was a hot day,' Mandy recalled. 'There were flies and gnats all over the place.'

'Awful nuisance. They even get into my operating theatre.' An intrusion so outrageous to Sir Clarence as to seem amusing.

'I'd the window of my cubicle open, when I was getting over the op. I was bitten by one, it made a huge red lump, just here.' Mandy displayed the back of her hand.

'That's funny! So was I,' said Sophie. 'The thing bit me on my neck. I couldn't wear my nice new necklace for a week, it was so sore. But it wasn't a gnat, it was a great mosquito.'

'Mosquitoes? Buzzing about our day-care department?' Sir Clarence looked offended.

'Definitely mosquitoes,' Sophie told him. 'I know, because I slapped it and killed it. It was the biggest mosquito I've seen in my life.'

'Me too. It was as big as a butterfly,' Mandy corroborated.

'Have you come far?' Sir Clarence asked, becoming impatient with flea bites. 'You must let the hospital provide your transport home. Sister will arrange it, won't you, Sister? I am so sorry you have had such a disturbing visit. Good morning.'

St Swithin's stood them a taxi. They got inside, pushchairs folded, babies on their laps sucking their dummies and quietly observing the traffic.

'There's a million in this for us,' said Mandy gleefully. 'Maybe millions.'

Sophie stared. 'I don't understand.'

'You will, luv, you will. Millions and millions! Oh, lovely, lovely, lovely! Oh, money, money, money! Millions and millions and millions!'

'I just want my right baby back,' Sophie said tearfully. She added pathetically, 'Whatever he looks like.'

Mandy's eyes gleamed. 'You and me must have a little talk.'

Sophie said nothing. But a mention of millions is inspiring. She invited impulsively, 'All right. Why don't you and your husband come and have dinner with us tomorrow?'

'He's working at dinner-time, luv.'

'We don't dine till eight.'

'Oh, you mean supper? That'ud be lovely.'

What quicksands of intimacy was she stepping upon? wondered Sophie. At least she hadn't called it high tea.

5

HUGO WAS DELAYED at St Swithin's that Monday evening by an emergency appendix, a sixteen-year-old girl, a private patient sent by her GP in Chelsea. As he left the Nightingale building, he encountered Sir Clarence standing alone in the lobby inside the front door. This was a small space with a circular desk in the middle, occupied most of the day by a smart female in a raspberry-coloured shirt and bow, who collected the cash and credit cards (bills had to be settled before leaving). And a man dressed like a US summertime cop, who eyed the screens from the TV cameras at all the building's apertures, the loot from private blocks being more desirable and plentiful than from the NHS.

'Clarence, I sent you a circular inviting subscriptions to the fund I'm getting up, for a memorial to Sir Lancelot Spratt,' Hugo reminded him pleasantly.

'Oh ... yes, of course, Hugo ... yes, yes,' Sir Clarence answered distractedly. 'Put me down for ten pounds ... for a hundred pounds. ...'

His eyes searched the deserted lobby.

'Something most peculiar happened to me today,' he confided hoarsely.

Hugo politely raised his eyebrows.

'Two mothers appeared at the post-natal clinic, claiming we'd mixed up their babies.'

'Oh, there was a case in the paper—'

'Yes!' he hissed. 'Every patient in the hospital has read it.'

'Well, it can be less disastrous giving mothers the wrong babes than giving them the wrong drugs, surely?' Hugo consoled him.

'But these were peculiar babies. Most odd. They were identical. Absolutely. You couldn't tell one from the other.'

'Like the Bedser twins, once bowling for Surrey,' recalled Hugo, a keen follower of the noble game, who had scored a century on the Close at Rugby.

'And they were somehow far advanced for their age. You expected them to ask for sweeties. To demand seeing videos of *Snow White and the Seven Dwarfs*. We've no record of how it all happened, but I'm confident we're in the clear. Anyway, I dislike freaks. They bobble on the smooth streams of science. You don't know what to do about them.'

'It may be some disorder of infant psychology,' Hugo suggested vaguely. 'I'll have a word with Alice when I get home.'

'She's putting up for that consultant's job here? When old Gus retires? Good! It would be splendid to have Alice as a colleague. I'll put in a good word for her, wherever I can.'

It was a promise Sir Clarence frequently made, because he

liked to suggest the influence which he had; but rarely effected, from fear of possibly compromising himself.

'Now I'm taking a taxi for a drink at my club,' he announced at the glass front door. 'I feel I deserve it. Thank God, no one important is on the boil tonight,' he dismissed labour among the upper classes.

'I've brought a Chinese take-away from Tum Tum's,' Hugo announced as he reached home in Dulwich after ten. 'Save you the bother of cooking anything.'

'Hugo, how lovely of you,' purred Alice.

She was younger, slim, good-looking, presenting a thick fringe of black hair snipped with surgical precision. She wore her evening jeans and St Swithin's T-shirt, relaxed in the sitting-room beside the semi-circular brick grate with the unlit coal effect gas fire, reading *The British Journal of Psychiatry*. She was an ambitious senior registrar, striding the crazy paving of the psychiatric department at St Swithin's.

They kissed passionately.

'It's wonderful you're back. You must be weary.'

She stroked his cheek tenderly. She was a wife loving to verging on the psychotherapeutic.

'Must build up the private practice,' Hugo said cheerfully. 'Though I must say, it's taking a time to get started. Do you realize, I've been a consultant now for over two years, and hardly make enough to pay for the new Merc? But I suppose Sir Lancelot had to bide a while, before half fashionable London was expecting him to stick his knife into them.'

'GPs simply can't be bothered to change patients from their

favourite surgeons, however over-patronised they are.' She ran her fingers through the wispy beard.

'That's true,' Hugo agreed resignedly. 'This one was sent by my old pal Sandy, who's started as GP off the King's Road. Good luck to him. We St Swithin's men must stick together.'

'Even if there's no St Swithin's?'

Hugo sighed. 'We'll all have to work at Bart's or Guy's or Tommy's or some other utterly inhospitable hospital. Perhaps I should make Sir Lancelot's memorial portable?' he reflected. 'So I can take it with me.'

They ate the take-away at the pine table in the breakfasting kitchen, which was also the lunching kitchen, the dining kitchen and the snacking kitchen. They had a small brand-new, outrageously expensive, terrace house beside Dulwich Park. It had three floors of immaculate rooms, connected by highly polished oak stairs, awaiting the yet unpredicted patter of tiny feet.

They used chopsticks on the soup-plated mess without second thought, everyone in Dulwich being sensitive to social correctitude. Hugo opened a bottle of Puligny-Montrachet, as he enjoyed the useful belief that inedible food needed drinkable wine.

He told her about Florence Nightingale.

'It was fascinating. You know how I read her up, because of the Sidney Herbert connection? All those biographies! One of half-a-dozen volumes. And this patient looked exactly like her.'

Alice gently diagnosed an illusion caused by a powerful desire to see it.

'I'm sure it wasn't an illusion,' he objected.

'I'm sure it was. You've been searching for this face for years, and had an emotionally determined illusion. It's quite common.'

'Like the Loch Ness Monster, you mean?'

'That's a mass illusion.' She deftly gathered the bamboo-shoots. 'Exacerbated by Scottish commerce.'

'Anyway, I'm seeing her again before tomorrow's rehearsal. I thought I might use her somehow in the Save St Swithin's campaign. But if I wasn't seeing straight, I suppose there's no point,' he trailed off, letting a pancake roll slip from grasp.

'I was reading your *Hamlet*, waiting for you to come home.' She pecked at the sweet-and-sour. 'I'm dreadfully bad on the classics. I haven't read any since my O-Levels at Cheltenham Ladies'. He does use a lot of clichés.'

'Clichés?'

'I made a list of them.' Alice drew a reversed supermarket check-out bill from her pocket. ' "For this relief much thanks . . . words, words, words . . . get thee to a nunnery . . . the lady doth protest too much . . . shuffled off this mortal coil. . . ." There' s one almost every page. You'd have thought a writer of Shakespeare's ability would have avoided them. I must mention it to your father, next time we go for lunch.'

'I shouldn't bother.' He glanced at the kitchen clock. 'I must learn my part. Shall I keep on the beard, to play it?'

'It seems a pity to shave it off, after all the fuss you made growing it.'

Hugo went to his study, a small room overlooking the tiny back garden. He turned on the light, sat at his desk, and opened the *Hamlet* paperback.

He had already got as far as Act I Scene 5.

Another part of the platform.
Enter GHOST *and* HAMLET.

HAM.	Where wilt thou lead me? speak; I'll go no further.
GHOST	Mark me.
HAM.	I will.
GHOST	My hour is almost come,
	When I to sulphurous and tormenting flames
	Must render up myself.
HAM.	Alas, poor ghost!

He decided to skip a bit.

HAM.	Murder!
GHOST	Murder most foul. . . .

He wondered if Alice had spotted that one. Cut to cue: '. . . strange and unnatural'.

HAM.	Haste me to know't, that I, with wings as swift
	As meditation or the thoughts of love,
	May sweep to my revenge.

Hugo closed his eyes tight and declared: 'Haste me to know't, that I with . . . with . . . wings of love . . . damn!' He glanced quickly at the page. 'Wings as swift as meditation or the thoughts of love . . . love . . . may sweep to my . . . my whatever.'

He decided to move on. Cut long speech by Ghost to cue: 'adieu, adieu! Hamlet, remember me' and Exit.

> HAM. O all you host of heaven! O earth! what else?
>   And shall I couple hell? O, fie! Hold, hold, my heart;
>   And you my sinews, grow not instant old,
>   But bear me stiffly up. Remember thee!
>   Ay, thou poor ghost, while memory holds a seat
>   In this distracted globe. Remember thee!
>   Yea, from the table of my memory
>   I'll wipe away all trivial fond records,
>   All saws of books, all forms, all pressures past,
>   That youth and observation copied there;
>   And thy commandment all alone shall live
>   Within the book and volume of my brain,
>   Unmix'd with baser matter: yes, by heaven!

He closed his eyes again. He did fairly well until the second Remember thee!, though understandably replacing sinews with tendons.

'Yea, from the table of my something blow, winds, and crack your cheeks! rage! blow! you cataracts and hurricanoes, spout till you have drenched our steeples, drowned the cocks. . . . That was from *Lear* last year. Why the bloody hell did it come back to me now? I must have a word with Alice.'

The two-year-old wedding-present clock on the bookcase was approaching one. He was operating at nine. He marked the page and went upstairs.

Alice was asleep under the duvet, wearing his discarded shirt, with broad scarlet stripes of such intensity it was frightening his patients. He pulled on his bright blue boxer shorts with blazing suns, a Christmas present. He slipped into bed and turned off the lamp.

His mind refused to lower the curtain.

'Yea, from the table of my memory I'll wipe away all trivial fond records,' he buzzed intracranially. 'All saws of books, all forms, all pressures past, that . . . that . . . that. . . .' What came next? 'That flesh is heir to, 'tis a consummation devoutly to be wished.' Of course not! He had been utterly mad to have learned the 'To be, or not to be' soliloquy first.

He groped for the text beside the bedside lamp. 'Fuck.' Had left it downstairs.

He slipped from the duvet, tiptoed across the restricted bedroom and descended barefoot the oak steps.

He stopped. A light shone under his study door. He remembered distinctly switching the light off. It was a thin white light, flickering. The torch of one of the burglars, who at this hour outnumbered the wakeful population of Dulwich.

What to do? 999? Policemen arriving in howling cars and flashing blue, filling the house and accompanied by fierce dogs? He would never get any sleep before leaving for St Swithin's.

He coughed.

The light stayed. He coughed again, louder.

'I don't know who you are in there, but if you clear off by the same way you came in, I won't call the fuzz.'

'Come!' said a voice.

Hugo froze. His jaw fell once again. He grasped the stylish door-handle. He gulped. He opened the door. At his desk sat Sir Lancelot Spratt, with his half-moon glasses on, reading *Hamlet*.

'Do come in, dear boy, you must be chilly walking about in your underpants.'

Hugo bravely took a step.

'You're acting this at the students' dramatic society, I gather?' Sir Lancelot laid down the paperback. 'In my day, Shakespeare was their most laughable appearance on the boards after *Charley's Aunt*.'

Sir Lancelot stood up. He wore his black jacket and striped trousers. He glowed slightly. His main difference from life was that you could see through him.

'So they're shutting St Swithin's?'

A strange smell. Ether, an outdated pungent anaesthetic.

'You know about it?' Hugo managed to say.

'We all know about it. I was just talking to Lord Lister and Percival Pott. I decided to come down, though it's considered rather bad form. After all, if we all kept coming down, there wouldn't be any point in our going away in the first place, would there?'

'Glad to see you,' Hugo managed to assure him.

'You're getting this Florence Nightingale look-alike to raise funds for St Swithin's? Forgive my overhearing your conversation at dinner. Good idea. Every summer they help numerous charities in Coventry, with a horse carrying Lady Godiva.'

Sir Lancelot stared at the dark garden through the window, hands clasped behind him.

'Florence is a decent woman, if a bit of a pain. We get on pretty well together. I've dealt with more difficult nursing sisters than her in the operating theatre. One used to slap the instruments red-hot into my gloved palm. Florrie's a good nurse – her *Notes on Nursing* contain as much common sense as my own lectures. But she isn't just a nurse, she's an effective politician. All her life, she knew exactly what she wanted, and exactly how to get it. That's the political art. If she were running the National Health Service, there'd be no trouble.'

'I'm sure,' Hugo agreed.

'Perhaps if you gingered up the Save St Swithin's campaign, you could scare the health minister? Politicians usually regard hospitals as sacred edifices. Whenever a politician is accused of some wild extravagance, his opponents always trot out how many hospitals it would have built. God knows what we should do with them, without any doctors to put inside.'

'You may care to know, Grandpa,' said Hugo, recovering himself in the ghostly affability, 'that I'm raising a memorial to you in St Swithin's.'

'How very kind.'

'If I can get enough money for it,' he admitted. 'Ay, there's the rub,' he found himself adding.

'I suppose, like Christopher Wren at St Paul's, you could inscribe "If you seek his monument, look round", on a stone in the middle of Golders Green cemetery?' Sir Lancelot gave a spectral chuckle. 'Though rather than becoming a pigeon perch, I'd prefer that you founded a Spratt Scholarship in practical surgery.'

'It shall be done,' said Hugo promptly, wondering how much scholarships worked out at.

'Perhaps you could create interest in the project – in a hospital that seems tactlessly to have totally forgotten me – through my gall-stone.'

Hugo was puzzled.

'It's in the pathology museum. I donated it, when Stuffy Rogers removed it for me early in the war. It's still there, despite the bombs and the repeated reorganizations. Specimen No. 66588, in the abdominal organs section.'

'I'll look it out tomorrow afternoon, Grandpa.'

'Good. How did England do at Lord's last summer?'

'We lost.'

'Oh? I'll have a word with W.G. I'll be keeping an eye on things.'

He melted into air, into thin air.

Hugo stumbled upstairs in the dark, banging into the bedroom door.

'What's the matter?' cried Alice, switching on the light.

'You look as though you've seen a ghost.'

'I have.'

'Not Florence Nightingale again?'

'No. Sir Lancelot Spratt. I had a long conversation with him.'

'But you've only been away a minute. I felt you get out of bed and looked at the luminous clock.'

'I can't have been a minute,' he said resentfully. 'We chatted about St Swithin's, his memorial, Florence Nightingale, cricket. You must have dozed off.'

'I certainly didn't. Only a minute's gone by, I assure you. Enough for you to slip down and pick up that book.'

He sat heavily on the bed. There was silence.

'Poor Hugo.' She softly stroked around his umbilicus. 'Seeing things, aren't you? But don't worry, it's not serious.'

'I'm *not* seeing things! I saw Florence Nightingale and Sir Lancelot only because they were there to be seen.'

'Almost everybody has illusions, at some time or another,' she told him gently. 'An illusion is only the misinterpretation of a stimulus. Walking in the dark, generations of people have misinterpreted shadows, trees, lamp-posts and so on, as human beings or wild animals.'

Hugo said nothing.

'Illusions often occur just when you're dropping off, dear. They are known as "hypnogogic". Or when you are just waking up, when they are known as "hypnopompic".'

Hugo still said nothing.

'I noticed from your Shakespeare bookmark, you were

learning your conversation with a ghost. Understandably, ghosts were on your mind.'

'If Sir Donald Sinden plays Hamlet, do you suppose he sees ghosts in the Garrick Club?'

'Illusions are connected with depressive states, you know, and feelings of guilt.'

'I have no feelings of guilt, nor do I deserve any,' he told her.

'Well! That's good to hear. But you have been a bit low recently, my darling. I'll bring you some Prozac from the hospital tomorrow.' She flicked her fingers invitingly. 'Come to bed.'

When Hugo at last felt sleepy, he remembered that he had forgotten to tell Amanda that the cholecystectomy was definitely on that morning.

6

AFTER THE OPERATING list that Tuesday, Hugo encountered Amanda Crockett-Jones again while waiting at six o'clock at a small table in the corner of the students' bar. It was the hour he had fixed with Marigold Peacock.

'Angels and ministers of grace defend us!' he was muttering. 'Be thou a spirit of health or goblin damn'd, why the sepulchre, wherein we saw thee quietly inurn'd, hath oped his ponderous and marble jaws – I've left out a huge chunk, I know it.'

He opened his eyes to see Amanda emerging from the students' common-room. The bar was a small, tatty room on a corner of the medical school building, furnished with a few blue plastic chairs and some well-ringed formica tables. Behind the counter was a shirt-sleeved member of the wine committee, a dignified title which the students rightly interpreted as their most enthusiastic boozers.

'What are you doing here?' Hugo asked. She was not a convivial consultant.

'I've been chairing a meeting of WHAMS, darling. Most gratifyingly positive. It's essential to tell the young what these organizations are all about. Most of them think we're just a collection of androphobic lunatics.'

Hugo made no comment.

'What are *you* doing here?' she countered.

'I'm waiting to give a young female an audition.'

'Why that snooker-ball in a glass case?'

'It's Sir Lancelot Spratt's gall-stone.'

A large shiny orange stone was teed-up on a brown cone of bakelite, the plastic of the 1930s. The case base bore a silver label:

PRESENTED BY SIR LANCELOT SPRATT FRCS 1939

BETTER OUT THAN IN.

'Magnificent, isn't it?' Hugo asked.

'It would be, coming from Sir Lancelot.'

'I've just claimed it from the pathology museum, as a family heirloom.'

'What are you going to do with it?'

'Auction it.'

'What, at Sotheby's? It would fit in with a lot of modern art, I suppose.'

'I thought within the hospital. To raise cash for his memorial.'

'How much have you got so far, darling?'

'With a hundred promised from Clarence, I'm pushing five thousand quid. Though I expect Clarence will forget. He has an economical generosity. Anyway, I've abandoned the plan for a solid memorial. I'm in favour of a Spratt Scholarship.'

'Who gave you that idea?'

'Sir Lancelot himself, last night.'

Amanda looked confused. 'You mean, he came to you in a dream?'

Hugo nodded.

'How unpleasant. I don't know about scholarships at the business end, but won't you have to buy a wedge on the Stock Exchange, to provide a succession of poor scholars with their cornflakes?'

'Possibly. All I care is that Sir Lancelot would cheer the idea, now he's in the undiscover'd country for whose bourn they don't issue return tickets.'

Hugo's guest entered by the courtyard door.

'Who does she remind you of?'

'Florence Nightingale.'

'Thank you, Amanda, for saying that,' Hugo responded. 'I was beginning to doubt my casting talents.'

Amanda left as Marigold reached the table.

'I got dreadfully lost. I followed the porter's directions and ended in a room with a nurse advancing on me with a clipboard.'

Marigold had an orange juice, he a small Scotch. As he fetched them from the bar, she was looking curiously round the room.

'I'm afraid this isn't much of a place to ask a guest,' he apologized.

'It's fascinating, like finding yourself in some native

drinking-place, in some foreign city like Constantinople.'

'It's called Istanbul now, isn't it?'

'Is it?' She came briskly to business. 'And what have you asked me for?'

'I wondered if you'd like to do a little acting for me? For the best of causes, keeping St Swithin's open.'

'My only theatrical experience is nativity plays.'

'That doesn't matter. You'll only have to dress up. You won't need to open your mouth. It'll be for only ten minutes.'

'It doesn't sound a very big part.'

'There will be repeat performances, if you're a success. Let me explain. Once a month there's a meeting of the hospital management committee. I'm on it. I don't know why. Perhaps the name helped,' he suggested modestly. 'The next one is on Thursday, at ten o'clock. There'll be about twenty of us. The chairman is the senior surgeon and medical director of St Swithin's, Trevor Blewett. He is a man with opinions more forceful than his intellect, which is considerable.'

'I know the sort.'

'My theatrical connections are well known, and I think they've come to expect, now and then, a dramatic gesture from me. On St Valentine's Day, I brought large bunches of flowers for all our female members. They didn't seem to mind,' he reflected. 'Quite the opposite. I thought I'd introduce you at the start of the meeting dressed like Florence Nightingale. Complete with lamp. If they approved – and you agreed – we could make you a figurehead of the "Save St Swithin's" campaign. We could hand out your photograph

to the Press with the message: "Florence Nightingale Says
Save St Swithin's!" We could visit important places in the
City over lunchtime, collecting important signatures. Why,
you'd gather a crowd just walking along Cheapside. Our
supporters equipped with rattling tins could perform
highway robbery. Of course, you may not remotely have time
for all this, as you're busy with marital problems,' he ended
apologetically.

'On the contrary, it would take my mind off them. It sounds
quite fun.'

'How splendid! Of course, we shall make you a little
present.' What *did* you give anyone whose father owned a
bank? 'Do you like port?'

'The occasional glass.'

'Good! My grandfather left some 1939 Tawny port. He gave
up port after his gall-stone was removed. You shall have the
remaining bottles,' he informed her grandly.

'His was an abnormally large gall-stone,' she observed,
indicating the labelled specimen.

'Yes, it was. I'd like you to look like Florence Nightingale as
she was at Scutari. That's the famous military hospital in
Turkey, which she illuminated with her lamp.'

Marigold nodded. 'Yes, a large but peculiar building, with
a tall tower at each corner. Seen across the Bosphorus, it
resembles an upturned billiard-table.'

'You've been there?' he asked in surprise.

'I saw the picture in an old *Illustrated London News*. My
father's got some bound copies at Chiddingford. So lifelike,

those Victorian drawings! The pictures of Florence Nightingale welcoming the poor casualties from the Charge of the Light Brigade, lying in their litters, or hanging round their comrades' necks, are quite like the real thing.'

'Would you mind going to Garland's, the theatrical outfitters in St Martin's Lane? I have already confirmed that they have a Florence Nightingale costume; it was worn in a West End show. They'll put it on the bill for *Hamlet*.'

He gave painstaking instructions for her negotiating St Swithin's, without the bonnet on and in a long macintosh, meeting him just before ten, to be hidden in a small library outside the committee-room. He hoped fervently that she would not become lost; but even Florence Nightingale would have become lost in St Swithin's.

They parted, Hugo having an on-stage read-through of the gravedigger scene, which he sadly anticipated would raise unwanted remarks from the students in the first-night audience.

At that moment, Edwin Kingston was opening the magenta front door of his house in Islington. He had passed a day of distracted accountancy.

He had come back from the City the previous evening to discover Sophie lying on the sofa in tears. Jeremy was sitting on the floor, sucking his dummy and turning over the cardboard pages of a book depicting pigs, donkeys and parrots.

'What's the matter, darling?' Edwin had asked, more in alarm than concern.

'Something terrible. I said I was going to the hospital—'

He nodded impatiently.

'There was another woman there with a baby exactly like Jeremy.'

He frowned. 'What do you mean, *exactly*?'

'What I say,' she told him snappishly. 'They could have been twins. If I'd have brought the other baby home, you wouldn't have noticed.'

'What sort of woman?' he asked, confused.

'Nothing like me. Working class. You're meeting them in hospitals all the time. None of this would have happened if I'd been on private medical insurance,' she reflected sorrowfully.

'The premiums are rather bad value,' he reminded her expertly. 'What did the hospital say about it?'

She thought. What *had* the hospital said? Nothing much, for all the talking.

'They told us to come back on Friday week.'

'They didn't admit any mix-up?'

'You'd hardly expect them to.'

Edwin carefully placed his executive case against the repro bureau. 'I don't believe a word of it,' he said quietly.

'Edwin!' She sat up. 'You don't understand the terrible situation we're in. There are two Jeremys in the world. Two! Identical!' She jabbed a finger at their child, unconcernedly turning over animals. 'From different wombs. From different plonkers, for that matter. It's unbelievable.'

Edwin sat on the sofa and took her hand. 'You're over-wrought,' he informed her.

'Of course I am. The Mother of God would be overwrought in this situation.'

'You're sure you're not imagining it all?' he persisted gently.

'I wish I was! I wish I was!'

'I'm not blaming you in the slightest,' he told her fairly. 'Women in your difficult emotional situation – having a baby by a man not their husband, a baby who, perhaps under-standably, they are deeply attached to, make up fantasies about the whole discreditable episode. To say they were given the wrong baby by the hospital is perfectly believable. Particularly allowing for the slackness of the National Health Service. You're always reading of them cutting off the wrong bits and forgetting to turn on the oxygen. But two unrelated women with two similar babies? It's a bit much!'

'You'll think differently when you set eyes on the other baby.'

'I'm sure I shall,' he said more cheerfully. 'But I never shall. Shall I? So there you are!'

'The baby's coming with its parents for dinner tomorrow.'

'There there!' He patted her hand. 'There there!'

Jeremy carefully laid aside his book, stretched, and clutched the sofa to stand on his pink feet, still sucking his dummy.

'All right, all right,' Sophie had continued despairingly, rising and gathering the infant. 'I'd better put him to bed.

Otherwise, you'll get no dinner with *Comic Cuts*.'

She referred to their favourite television show, always top of the ratings; but their evening had touched a gloom beyond which even *Comic Cuts* could lighten.

The next day in his office, Edwin reflected that Sophie was a pathetically sensitive soul, who did not care for any irregularities at all in her domestic life. She should see her doctor, or perhaps more dramatically a psychiatrist, who would rationally analyse her guilt at deceiving her loving husband. Edwin remembered an accountancy colleague whose wife had suffered the fantasy of being Cleopatra. There had been difficulties procuring asses' milk for her bath, and the asps she wished to apply to her breast. He sought his colleague, and discovered that she had entered a private psychiatric clinic beside the upper Thames, and was now herself again. Edwin had the clinic's name and weekly rates in his mind, as he crossed the narrow hallway arriving home that Tuesday evening. He caught an unusually savoury smell, indicating dinner-party cooking.

'I'm arranging the Parma ham round the melon.' Sophie excused herself, from the kitchen beyond the small front dining-room.

Edward saw that table was laid normally for one of their dinner parties of four.

Sophie had passed the day in a state. Quite ridiculously, she told herself, she was more concerned about her entanglement in the cogs of social mechanics than by her crushing in the machinery of St Swithin's.

Should there be candles? she had pondered deeply. When Julia or Amelia and their husbands came for dinner, she always had candles on the table – pink or emerald or violet from Wax & Wix, in a pair of holders like little glass bowls, from Habitat. But would her outlandish guest – whom she had left with her Scott, or possibly her own Jeremy, on a corner in Hackney – be baffled by the necessity of candles in a house illuminated by normal electricity?

What should she give these social intruders to eat? She was proud of her boeuf Wellington, but the people (as politicians in the papers now called the working class) certainly did not appreciate rare beef, and would probably spit it out as uncooked. Steak-and-kidney pudding would be wiser, and her famed chocolate marquise with raspberry coulis, to be replaced by Black Forest. To drink? Cans of lager? Guinness? Supermarket plonk? Vodka seemed to dominate the commercials, and must have a usefully widespread following.

And the husband! Sophie shuddered. Would he be long-haired, ear-ringed, smoking – smoking! The stink! His only certainty was not resembling Mrs Miles's baby. Nor her own baby. There is nothing like the cocoon of social superiority to deflect mental torment; it sustained Oscar Wilde in Reading Gaol.

A couple whom you had invited to dinner could not possibly come if they did not exist, Edwin reflected, as he left the dining-room for the sitting–room, laid his executive case against the repro bureau and poured himself a gin and tonic, taking tongs to the ice. But if they really were a fantasy of

Sophie's, they were going to have an awful lot left in the fridge, not to mention the extra washing-up.

Sophie appeared in her pinny, wiping her hands on a dish-cloth printed with a Matisse.

'I've been thinking rationally about the Jeremy problem,' Edwin told her. Edwin thought rationally about every problem, down to the slices of toast he could consume healthily for breakfast. 'And I've come to a decision: we'll get him adopted. That'll solve everything.'

'But I don't want him adopted.'

He handed her a small gin and tonic.

'Why?'

'Because he's my baby.'

'But you said on Sunday you'd been sent home with the wrong one,' he accused her crossly. 'Like the two couples in the paper.'

'I wasn't sent home with the wrong one,' she told him forcefully. 'Neither was the other mother. I remember now. The hospital checked the records.'

'Listen,' he began in exasperation. 'If your baby looks like her baby – if it exists—'

'It *does* exist. Why do you suppose I've spent all day cooking steak-and-kidney pudding?'

'Steak-and-kidney pudding?' He raised his eyebrows appreciatively. One of his favourites, offered with uncharitable rarity. 'Then your baby must *be* her baby.'

'Her baby isn't her baby. It doesn't look a scrap like her, or like her husband. Her own mother's being absolutely horrid about it. She told me the whole story in the taxi from St Swithin's.'

'All right! We'll get both babies adopted. Somebody must be in the market for twins.'

'No. If I had him, I want to keep him.'

'You must be mad!' he exploded. 'Do you want to bring up a baby who looks nothing like you, but looks like some unspeakable man who's fathered another baby on the same night?'

'I don't think you understand women,' she dismissed the argument.

'What about me?' he demanded with rising anger. 'You expect me to love and cherish some other man's baby? To house him and rear him? To educate him, probably at some vastly overpriced public school? To prepare him for manhood? To keep him in idleness at a university? To buy him a car? To find him a job? To put up with his bloody girl-friends? Or bloody boyfriends,' he added, in ultimate horror.

'But he isn't another man's baby,' she protested. 'He couldn't be.'

'Tell that to the marines, who, as far as I am concerned, could have fathered him as a regimental exercise.'

'Now you're being obscene.'

He crossed to the drinks cabinet in the corner for another gin.

'If you won't have him adopted, I want a divorce,' he told her.

'Please yourself. This conversation has become too compli-cated.' She untied her pinny. 'We shall have to interrupt it, because they're here.'

Edwin looked through the window, while lifting his gin. He was struck motionless. A small, red, well-cleaned car was finding a space outside. A lanky man in jeans and a blue jumper emerged to assist a small woman in a purple blouse and brown check skirt to extract from the back a car-seat containing a baby sucking a dummy.

'Sophie—' Edwin croaked.

'Well, let them in.'

Edwin opened the front door. He stared at Scott. He felt that he had stumbled upon a blatant forgery of his own signa-ture on a cheque for several million.

'Come in,' he invited nervously.

'What a nice house,' said Mandy.

'I'm Jim,' said Jim.

Sophie reappeared from the kitchen without the pinny. She had taken advantage of utilizing a dress which Julia and Amelia had seen. Scott was tidied away upstairs, where Jeremy had accepted, with his usual considerate obedience, a premature beddy-byes. Edwin bemusedly opened the drinks cabinet. It was all horribly true. The men from Mars had appeared on his doorstep, asking for a vodka.

The woman was chatty. The man was affable. They sat on the sofa. Edwin paced about, pouring vodka. They sat down to the Parma ham and melon.

'Quickprice?' asked the man, sipping the wine knowledgeably. 'It's the supermarket I work in. One of their best bottles, good value.'

Mandy thought the candles were lovely.

'Let's get down to business,' said Mandy brightly, scraping clean her melon skin. 'Then we can all relax and enjoy.'

'But I don't see what we can do about this awful situation,' said Sophie plaintively. Neither couple had been eager to mention it until some thin bands of sociability were secured. 'The hospital are being so unhelpful. We'll have to wait ten whole days until finding out what they have to say.'

'That's fine,' said Mandy. 'It leaves time for the arithmetic. On Friday week, we'll tell them how much they owe us.'

'I don't follow,' said Edwin.

Sophie returned to the kitchen.

'Maybe you don't understand figures?' Mandy suggested. 'My dad taught me. He worked behind the counter in a betting shop.'

'I'm an accountant!' said Edwin crossly.

'Oh, luvley. That'll save us a lot of trouble.'

'My husband wants to have Jeremy adopted,' said Sophie. She placed the steak-and-kidney pudding, and equally solemnly, four of their best dinner-plates, on the sparklingly polished repro Chippendale table with the Portmeirion table-mats.

'Adopted?' exclaimed Mandy. 'You can't have him adopted.'

'Why not?' Edwin asked, still feeling offended.

'Because there's money in him,' said Mandy calmly. 'Loads

of money. Make them off-shore millionaires look like down-and-outs. Jim, you got my paper?'

Jim took a folded sheet from his trouser pocket while Edwin earnestly sliced into the pudding. What a delicious smell!

'Oo, steak-and-kidney, lovely.' Mandy spread out the paper covered with writing, pushing aside the Kingstons' wedding-present cutlery. 'I took Scott down to our public library yesterday afternoon in his buggy; they were all very nice, they keep the old newspapers, did you know?'

Edwin nodded, as Sophie presented the carrots Vichy.

'*The Times*. Do you read it?'

'Every day.'

'Oh, thanks, I love carrots. Listen to this—' Mandy pointed down the paper with her knife. 'Keyhole surgery errors, three-quarters of a million pounds. Pregnant womb removed, two million. Failed female sterilization and birth injuries, three million. Baby's finger cut off by mistake, three-quarters of a million. Failed vasectomy, only half a million. Death from the pill, eight million. These people are laughing all the way to the morgue,' she concluded, looking up with dark eyes glistening.

'Yes, I noticed the other day that just seeing someone else die was worth a hundred thousand,' Edwin said.

He was warming to her. His accountant's brain had instantly seen the point.

'Human suffering, it comes pricey,' Mandy decided. 'Quite right, too. There's a lot of it about.'

Edwin nodded agreement. Matters were becoming deserving of his attention.

'It's only just to compensate the victims of any malpractice or incompetence adequately,' he pronounced.

'That's right. They cut off your wrong leg, and it's like winning the pools. Go on a cruise, buy a Jag, live a life of idleness – who wants two legs anyway? They make lovely tin ones; a pal of my dad's used to take his off when he'd had a few, left it behind in pubs all over London.'

Sophie was noticing that Jim ate heartily with his elbows out, holding his knife like a pen. Oh, dear.

Sophie was beginning to wish that she had never assailed St Swithin's at all. She wished that she had never had a baby. She wished that she was incurably infertile.

'That's all very well, but what exactly has the National Health Service done to harm us?' she asked dampeningly.

'Exactly, we dunno. But they done something. Look – we went into hospital as two normal mothers, right? We got two babies who don't even look like our milkman. Least, mine don't.'

'We buy our milk at the supermarket,' Sophie told her briskly.

'And the babies are dead ringers. So somefink's gone wrong, annit? And if somefink's gone wrong in the hospital, they gotta pay for it. I reckon that session we had grunting and groaning last April could turn out the best day's work of our lives.'

'When we go to the hospital on Friday week, Sir Clarence

isn't going to produce his cheque-book,' said Sophie chill-ingly. She thought Mandy was becoming over-excited.

'That Sir Clarence I do not trust. He's as smooth as a car salesman. As for that O'Shea, our area's full of men like him. I wouldn't trust any of 'em, no more than I'd expect to find a four-leaf clover in a cress sandwich.'

'Very well. Then what's our next step?' asked Sophie. She noticed that even Edwin seemed animated by the popular attraction of easy money.

'Getting legal aid. It takes time, but it's not too difficult. Lots of our friends get legal aid, don't they, Jim?'

He nodded. 'Always a bit of skylarking round where we live. Cars, mostly.'

'Bloke next door was housebreaking for years, and we never knew it till the police came for him early one morning.'

'They broke his door down with a sledgehammer. Looked like a hundred of them in the street. You wouldn't believe the noise, woke everyone up.'

'Don't worry about the legal aspects.' Edwin was now smiling. 'I've a quicker route to justice. An old friend of mine's a solicitor in one of the most reputable firms in London. If the hospital's at fault, he'll find it, believe you me. In fact, I think he'd find a fault even if they aren't.'

Edwin set his knife and fork together on his empty plate.

'I can get hold of him tomorrow. He'd act on a "no win no fee" basis, of course. Do you understand what that is?'

'No,' said Mandy innocently, 'I'd have to ask a bookie.'

Sophie was serving the Black Forest. What funny afters, Mandy observed to herself.

'Do you take coffee after dinner?' Sophie asked. 'It's decaffeinated.'

'Please. Milk and sugar.'

'Only a quarter glass, I'm driving,' said Jim, as Edwin reached for the decanter. 'Next time you're in Hackney, use my branch of Quickprice and try the Chateau Draguinon – it's got a good nose, lovely palate and it's a special offer.'

7

THE GRAND COMMITTEE-ROOM at St Swithin's Hospital was a fitting monument to the stately practice of medicine in the mid-eighteenth century, when physicians wore snowy buckskin breeches, scarlet gilt-braided coats and lace ruffles, were bewigged like judges and sniffed regularly at gold-headed canes. These valuable handles were charged with a pungent vinegar to ward off omnipresent infections; the vinegar was ineffectual, and the doctors lived or died according to their luck, just like the recipients of their elaborate and often revolting treatments.

The committee-room was a vast apartment on the top of the oldest hospital building. It presented impressed visitors with a Marble-Arch fireplace, tall windows and a vaulted ceiling, and was hung with extravagantly framed paintings of notable St Swithin's practitioners. The walls between them were closely inscribed in gold leaf with the names of its benefactors, who had purchased immortality for themselves, and their occupations, at a most reasonable price. *Wm. Furbellow, Fruiterer, of Poultry, £5*, exists for ever behind the high chairman's seat at the massive committee-table, to which a pair of oaken limbs could be attached and extended across the parquet floor to accommodate wider opinions.

Here were made intelligent and stringent decisions on the hospital's performance until 1940, when the Luftwaffe invoked the restoration work performed in 1950. By then, the National Health Service had been alive for two years, engendering committees with such rabbity fertility that they were mostly crammed into undignified warrens in the basements, or into attics among the aldermanic City pigeons. But Mr Trevor Blewett, MS, FRCS, the medical director of St Swithin's, commanded the best setting for his powerful deliberations, during which he could pleasantly foresee himself one day on the wall in a gold frame, with 'Sir' starting the title line.

'There are two hundred and thirty-one shopping days until Christmas,' Mr Blewett began grimly that Thursday morning, to some twenty of the hospital's leading clinicians, administrators and financiers. 'But I can assure you, these will be hardly enough to make plans for the hospital's efficient functioning at that festive time of the year. I am going by the utter chaos that prevailed last winter, and provided the newspapers and television with such handy outraged material. We seemed to present them with more drama than these hundred hospital shows they put on every week.'

Someone gave a little laugh. Mr Blewett glared from the chairman's throne in the middle of the table. He was a burly, red-faced, bristly-haired man in a well-tailored suit and a vivid red tie. He was a close friend of the health minister –

which seemed to the committee a more certain means of keeping St Swithin's open than any resolutions under his chairmanship.

'It isn't funny. Not when we have sick people lying for hours on trolleys and stretchers in casualty, because the wards have become choked. Our emergency admissions at St Swithin's are seven per cent higher in the winter. They get worse than that if there is only a moderate flu epidemic, and even a short spell of icy weather for people to slip about on. We have staff shortages, because we are, unfortunately, not ourselves immune to illnesses. We have no money. We shall be in deficit this year, despite the £1.2 billion tip the government is slipping the Health Service. We are cutting our services, we are closing our wards, like fifteen per cent of the one hundred and nineteen other health service authorities. Our planning is so poor, we resemble the railways, who are traditionally surprised to discover that it snows in winter. I have therefore prepared a paper—'

He waved it at the professional men and women sitting passive-faced before him.

'Which you will have received with the agenda, giving my ideas to rectify this disgraceful incompetence.'

'Mr Chairman—' interrupted Hugo, at the far end of the long table.

Mr Blewett glared.

'What's the matter?'

'Before we start the serious discussion of your paper, may I mention a subject of importance?'

Hugo shifted on his seat, one eye on the shut oak doors at the end of the room. Marigold had not arrived. Perhaps she had funked it. Good thing, possibly, with Trevor Blewett in this mood.

'A memorial scholarship I am founding for Sir Lancelot Spratt.'

Mr Blewett looked shiftily along the lines of faces. Sir Lancelot was not portrayed in the grand committee-room, because he had had a row about his posture with the hospital's selected artist, who hurled his palette at him, ruining his suit. But his name, like Churchill in the Commons, demanded attention and respect.

'Go on,' he grunted to Hugo.

'I hope you can persuade all your colleagues to contribute. And, of course, contribute yourselves,' Hugo added, with a glance at Mr Blewett, who had not. He wondered desperately how to waste more time. 'On Friday evening, at six o'clock, I am auctioning Sir Lancelot's gall-stone in this room—'

Everyone looked curious.

'I found it in the pathology museum, where I'm sure it was instructive to the students. I hope it will raise a tidy sum.'

Nobody said anything.

'Let's get on,' said Mr Blewett.

Hugo stood abruptly and left. The pleasant-looking female physician beside him wondered if he was offended. Mr Blewett wondered if he wanted a pee. Outside, Hugo found Marigold.

'I was stopped by the porter,' she explained calmly. 'He

seemed to think I was some sort of demonstration. He kept telephoning people. I am usually never late for anything.'

'Follow me.' Hugo gulped nervously. 'Good luck.'

Hugo for a moment faced the wide double doors, then threw them open. Everyone turned, startled. Before them stood Marigold, a white lace cap across the back of her head and puffed over her ears, a lace collar, a black neckband secured with a jewelled brooch, a dark grey dress with a braided front, more braid running in three hoops down to the hem of her long, full skirt. Her face was expressionless. In her right hand she held an Aladdin's lamp, extracted from the panto section of Garland's.

Silence. Then the committee smiled, laughed, clapped, or called at Hugo: 'We know who it is!'

'Not play-acting again?' Mr Blewett complained wearily. 'Last month, you didn't have to put on a chef's hat and a French accent to discuss the hospital cooking.'

'Whatever we discuss – if St Swithin's no longer exists – is pointless,' Hugo pointed out. 'I think Miss Nightingale can help to keep us open. She will become our valuable logo.'

Marigold followed Hugo into the room.

'But the likeness is supernatural,' exclaimed the pleasant physician. 'Can't she stay a minute? So we can have a better look at her?'

Marigold sat, sweeping her skirt, in a chair which Hugo had kept empty beside him. She picked up Mr Blewett's paper from the table, and perused it calmly.

'Can't she recite something?' suggested a psychiatrist from

the end of the table, giggling. 'Perhaps *The Charge of the Light Brigade*?'

'We've got a full agenda—' began Mr Blewett.

'Oh, come on!' urged most of the committee, clearly feeling that so remarkable a spectacle must be enjoyed, if briefly.

'Well, whatever you're going to do, don't take long about it,' he told her. 'We're all busy.'

Marigold addressed the committee in a clear, even voice.

'Pressures upon St Swithin's, and all other hospitals, become severe between mid-December and the end of February. They reach their peak between December 30 and January 20. These figures have been obtained from a survey of the eight NHS regions.'

'I know all that.' Mr Blewett looked awkward. 'I don't know why I omitted it from my own paper.'

'The figures have only just become available,' said Marigold tolerantly, looking him in the face. 'Nevertheless, it is the hospital's obligation to provide for its patients the same service as in midsummer.'

'Naturally, I agree with that,' said Mr Blewett. 'The obvious question is, how?'

'Miss Nightingale will tell you.' Hugo wrapped his arms round himself with suppressed glee. The act was enjoying unexpected success.

'It would be effective to employ extra staff, to open extra wards, but this would cost hundreds of thousands of pounds which we do not have,' said Marigold.

'I agree with that wholeheartedly,' said Mr Blewett, and

someone called: 'Hear, hear!'

'It is essential to be clear about our objectives.'

Marigold put her hands together and stared round the table.

'First, there must be no closure of the accident and emergency department. It was closed last year, and that was an unworthy capitulation. I arrived at Scutari shortly after the Charge of the Light Brigade.'

She eyed the psychiatrist, who looked startled.

'The one thousand and fifty casualties arrived by the shipful. They were those officers and men who had survived the voyage across the Black Sea, and not been thrown overboard with the dead horses. Room had to be made for them in the wards of the Selinine Quicklaci barracks, which the British Army had converted to a hospital by the simple measure of whitewashing the walls. The wards were no more than long corridors, with no lighting, and I had to make my nightly rounds carrying a lamp.'

'That very one, I suppose?' smiled a male paediatrician.

'No, I used a linen Turkish Army one, like a candle in a Chinese lantern. This one is only my symbol.'

Hugo had told her about the lamp, but he shifted uneasily in his chair. Why did she have such vivid knowledge of Scutari? Come to think of it, how had she instantly recognized that specimen in the students' bar as a gall-stone? Perhaps she was really a failed medical student? The committee were looking at her with uncanny attention. Mr Blewett was looking like a surgeon with a kidney just come off in his hand.

'I went round selecting those patients already in the wards but who were well enough to leave the hospital. There were a surprising number of them. Many were lingering to enjoy the food and comfort, and avoid return to active service. I obtained their discharge from Sir John Hall, the medical Inspector-General, who was across the sea at Balaklava. He somewhat surprisingly granted this, being overwhelmed with casualties and ready to do absolutely anything to cope with them. Later, of course, my position became established, and I discharged what patients I wished. As frequently as I had, unfortunately, to bury them.'

What a performance! thought Hugo.

'Your position in a military hospital must have been diffi- cult,' Mr Blewett ruminated.

'I had one advantage: I could not be court-martialled. So I could raid the quartermaster's stores, break all regulations, and defy everybody.'

'Bravo!' A male orthopaedic surgeon at the end of the table laughed and clapped.

'Patients not well enough to return to their regiments I installed in a large house nearby, taking particular care that they had the best attention of my nurses and orderlies. We must do the same here at St Swithin's next winter,' Marigold directed simply.

'Do what?' demanded Mr Blewett.

'When those who are falling sick pour in, those who are getting better must move out.'

'Yes, Miss Nightingale,' Mr Blewett insisted. 'Or whoever

you are. But the problem is, they *cannot* be discharged. They still need treatment. They have not got the army, with its duty to take care of them. They have poor homes, or no homes, and there is no one whatever to look after them. Or at least, there is no one whatever who wants to.'

'Naturally, I am aware of that,' she told him quietly. 'Thus, I suggest a limited number of medical, nursing and auxiliary staff be detailed to attend these discharged patients, in homes of their own which are tolerable – most of them, I suspect. Vans would be requisitioned from the police to transport them with some urgency. They have blue lights and sirens to get about the streets, which would impress the public with the effort that the NHS is making. The patients must be seen by medical staff four-hourly, if their sickness demands it. After all, maternity cases now spend six hours in hospital, then are seen twice daily at home by the midwife, and do perfectly well.'

'Would it work?' asked Mr Blewett gloomily. 'We hear a lot of these bright ideas.'

'I would be confident of managing such a service. It should be popular with the patients. Nobody wishes to remain in a hospital, or any institution, when they can return to their own bed or fireside.'

'True,' Mr Blewett agreed.

Hugo was growing alarmed. Her historical character-building had come across enthrallingly, but the act was getting out of hand.

'I am generally successful with my plans,' Marigold

asserted calmly. 'A nearby house, possibly a halfway house for drug addicts, possibly a school, a geriatric home, or small hotel, would temporarily shelter patients with no homes. Medical care, without question, arriving regularly.'

'You'd never get the social service and housing people, not to mention the hotel owners, to agree,' argued Mr Blewett.

'*I* should,' she told him quietly. 'There is a way of appealing for the welfare of the sick over the head of officialdom, which is irresistible. Surely the size of *The Times*'s fund raised for Crimean casualties – thirty thousand pounds in 1855 – is proof enough? Human values in such matters do not change, if the bleak facts are put before human eyes. The over-crowding of St Swithin's Hospital in winter must be presented not as a technical failure of the NHS, but as a national, and inhumane, disaster,' she ended firmly.

Mr Blewett slapped the table. 'That's exactly the way to go about it.'

'Hear, hear!' said several committee members loudly.

'For a start, I can shift the blame from St Swithin's,' Mr Blewett told them, pocketing the plan. 'The bed crisis will be a national challenge, like the Falklands War, the Crimean War for that matter. We shan't have to pick the newspapers from the doormat all winter trembling with apprehension. Good idea, Miss Nightingale! I'll pass it on to the minister.'

'But patients in winter may not wish to be tumbled out of our nice warm, comfortable, well-fed and well-serviced hospital,' objected the pleasant female physician.

Marigold eyed her sharply. 'A hospital is good for the seriously ill alone. Otherwise it becomes a lodging-house where the nervous become more nervous, the foolish more foolish, the idle and selfish more selfish and idle. Where there is no higher interest in life, illness naturally becomes an amusement and a luxury. If nothing occupies a woman more than her dinner and her mucous membrane, her mucous membrane and her dinner will become her sole object. To breakfast in bed, and to be pitied, her sole solace. Does that answer your question?'

'Er, I think so,' said the pleasant physician.

'Another solution we must remember is mobility. In Constantinople, I was four thousand miles from home, by sea. In our own island, nobody can be more than four hundred miles from home, anywhere. If we have no hospital beds in London, and empty beds in Aberdeen, we must use them.'

'Last winter, we had to find beds for our patients as far off as Newcastle or Leeds,' Mr Blewett objected. 'Which to most of them are only the names of football teams. It wasn't popular.'

'Modern transport, by air or by road, would reduce the journey to what was an unnoticeable duration in my day.'

Marigold continued her lecture, hands clasped loosely on the table.

'We must pay for the relatives to travel with them, and to stay in the area. The cost would be comparatively slight. Most importantly, we must assert the doctrine that valuable treatment can be offered away from home, and that the site is irrelevant. It is like a battle. The wounded soldier is removed from dressing-station to base hospital. The civilian from our busy casualty departments to peaceful places where there are plenty of people waiting to treat him. This is the image which must be impressed upon the public. If done skilfully, it will be accepted.'

'By the right, quick march!' said a male throat surgeon.

'The next item on the agenda,' Marigold continued, in a businesslike way, raising the paper, 'is, I see, cross-infection in hospitals. It is clearly a perversity, to retain patients in hospital for an infection which they have incurred in the hospital itself. It may seem a strange principle to enunciate, but the very first requirement of a hospital is that it should do the sick no harm.'

'Quite right,' nodded Mr Blewett.

'Hear, hear!' rang round the table.

'I must confess that I never believed in the evil, or even the existence, of microbes,' Marigold continued, 'until Sir Almroth Wright's inoculations so effectively prevented typhoid fever among our troops in the war of 1914. I could do nothing with typhoid or cholera but apply abdominal stoops.'

'But Miss Nightingale,' laughed a male transplant surgeon. 'In 1914 you had been dead four years.'

'So I had. Forgive me. At Scutari, I achieved mastery of the microbes by scrubbing out the dirt they lived in. My gentlefolk ladies from England, I set to work with the scrubbing-brush and at the wash-tub, though they had voyaged to Turkey with romantic notions of clasping soldiers' fevered brows. Pus and infection fell at once.'

'Our cleaning ladies do a perfectly good job,' objected Mr Blewett grumpily.

Hugo stood. The show had gone on long enough.

'I hope my joke hasn't confused the committee?' he apologized all round.

'No, we've enjoyed it,' said the male orthopaedic surgeon.

'Better than television,' smiled a female obstetrician.

'Miss Nightingale will exit.'

They walked to the door to a round of vigorous applause.

'A wonderful performance!' exclaimed Hugo, outside.

'I'm glad they seemed to like it,' Marigold said modestly.

'You changed Trevor Blewett's thinking, which I've never succeeded in managing myself,' he told her feelingly. 'Where did you get all those statistics?'

'I rummaged in the Social Services Research Centre library yesterday afternoon. And I picked up a paperback on Florence Nightingale's life.'

They left along the main corridor of the St Swithin's old block.

'There's a pound for you,' smiled a passing middle-aged woman, pressing a coin into Marigold's hand.

'Thank you.'

'What are you collecting for?'

'Oh – medicine in general,' said Marigold.

'It's a lovely dress.'

'Thank you.'

Someone else gave her 10p.

They reached the great gate, where Hugo had enticed a

dozen Press photographers and a crew from Gigantic TV News. Passers-by gawped briefly – it is common in London streets to see people doing something for the telly.

'Look, I've a stockbroker friend with an office in Poultry,' Hugo told her. 'Could you meet me there tomorrow at noon? I've fixed some other offices round the City, Bevis Marks and Threadneedle Street and so on. We'll get valuable support from City bigwigs for saving St Swithin's. But you're sure you can spare the time?' He stopped apologetically.

'My life at the moment is empty. My former husband has quietly escaped. He has found another woman. I hope with a nice home, because he is extremely fond of his creature comforts.'

Hugo found her a taxi. Returning to the courtyard, he halted abruptly. He did not want to rejoin the meeting. It would be like standing on stage when the show had closed. Her performance was so realistic, it was eerie. He went to the medical school library instead, and sat in a dim corner inattentively reading *The Journal of Medical History*.

At two o'clock he was operating. At six, he was sitting in the coffee-room in the theatre suite, wearing a blue, short-sleeved V-neck singlet and trousers, a green cap, a white mask round his neck, and white wellies. It was a small room lined with tall green lockers, and he sat on a white plastic chair against an oblong low table scattered with journals and forms, writing up notes. The other coffee-drinker was Amanda, wearing her own set of theatre blues.

'Dr Crockett-Jones—' The smiling head of a black nurse, in

a theatre cap and dangling mask, appeared round the door. 'Could you have a peep at that last patient of yours in recovery?'

Amanda put down her cup and left by the door, Sir Lancelot entered through its woodwork. He wore theatre blues and cap, half-moons on his nose. Hugo could see through him. He looked up from his notes, unalarmed, even unfazed. He supposed Horatio felt the same, the second time he met the Ghost of Hamlet's father.

'No mask?' he smiled.

'I don't need one. I don't breathe. You did the pancreatectomy excellently, dear boy. I was watching over your shoulder. A difficult one, I should not at all have liked doing it myself.'

'Thank you.'

'Then you made an utter balls-up of a right inguinal hernia.'

'I know. And I did the op to show the students.'

'Whenever you do any operation to show the students, it always goes wrong. That anaesthetist of yours is pretty bossy, isn't she?'

'She's highly efficient, which is all that counts.'

'I suppose she must be efficient, to follow that array of flashing numbers. I started surgery with a rag-and-bottle man, rag in one tail-coat pocket, bottle of chloroform in the other, everything monitored by his finger-tips. I never had a moment's worry.'

'Coffee, Grandpa? Digestive biscuit?' Hugo offered politely.

'No, we don't use those sort of things. Is she suffering from the Lesbos disease? There's a lot of it about.'

'Amanda! She's had a dozen live-in boyfriends. She cracks men like walnuts.'

'I see. I just saw Clarence Strangewood in the theatre suite. Got gonged, didn't he?'

Hugo nodded.

'Good luck to him. I used to fish with his father. Clarence struck me as looking like his father when he'd got his line in a tangle.'

'He's worried about two abnormal cases. Rather scary ones. Please don't buzz it about—'

'I am as silent as a ghost, I assure you.'

'He has two mothers who were delivered on the same day, a year ago, of identical male babies. They're growing up so fast that they should be riding little tricycles, as far as I could make out.'

'Ah!' Sir Lancelot looked serious. He sat on a plastic chair and rubbed his beard thoughtfully. 'There's been a lot of chat up there—' He nodded skywards. 'About the biological engineering of human machines. All identical, like the original T-model Fords. Which means the end of the human race as we know it and love it. Charles Darwin is having fits. All mothers will give birth to these machines, instead of ordinary babies. It's something to do with dominant genes. If they're all the same sex, the end of the world is nigh, *ergo*. Not that I care, it's dreadfully crowded up there already.'

Hugo looked aghast. 'But surely! No geneticist alive could

THE LAST OF SIR LANCELOT

produce a result like that. Or would ever want to.'

'I don't want to be a spectre of doom, but yes.'

Hugo shrugged. He supposed in Sir Lancelot's environment there floated beings who could ponder the future like the past.

'What are the prospects for England with Strongi'th'arm, that young fast bowler for Yorkshire?' Sir Lancelot enquired.

'Well, he's got a murderous leg-cutter.'

'That's good news. I might drop into Lord's next summer. It would be good to wear my MCC tie again. How's my memorial fund going?'

'Slowly.'

He vanished. Amanda came in.

'It wasn't my patient, Hannah's there already.'

She sat down.

'I hope your coffee isn't cold?'

She look puzzled. 'Cold? I've only been away half a minute.'

'No you haven't! At least ten minutes.'

Smiling, she passed him the hot mug. 'Look at the clock,' she advised.

Hugo glanced at the second hand. He had observed the clock on the wall as she left. She was right.

He picked up the folders of notes.

'I'll finish these tomorrow. I'm going home.'

'What *is* the matter with you?' Amanda looked concerned. 'When I went out, you were making jokes about the disastrous hernia.'

'Migraine,' he said quickly. 'With flashing lights in front of my eyes.'

He energetically mimed flicking them away.

'I didn't know you got migraine.'

'Neither did I. But I do now.'

'Shall I send an orderly to get you some Migraleve from pharmacy?'

'No. I think it's psychopathic. Alice will be keen to treat it when I get home.'

'Yes, she would be.'

He left.

He arrived back in Dulwich, to kiss Alice passionately. She stood in her St Swithin's shirt and jeans, stirring mince in a Le Creuset saucepan. He reached into a corner cupboard, and poured a large whisky. It was also the drinking kitchen.

'Peculiar things are happening at the hospital. No, I haven't killed anyone. The worst I did was messing up a hernia. Listen.'

She obediently turned off the mince and sat opposite. He told her of Florence Nightingale's realistic performance, which had gripped the committee. Of the materialization of Sir Lancelot. And he added for effect the identical babies.

'Sir Clarence was always anxious about his patients,' she stated. 'And his anxieties are getting worse.'

Hugo nodded. 'Yes, now they're even extending from his private patients to his NHS ones.'

'This Florence Nightingale person was obviously playing to the gallery,' Alice dismissed her. 'And you don't *really* believe that you saw your grandfather, do you?'

'I tell you, he was as real as that Aga in the corner.'

'Poor, dear, lovely lamb,' she purred. She held his hands in hers on the pine table. 'Did you take your Prozac?'

'No. I don't believe in drugs. No surgeons do.'

'You know what you need?' she continued in the same soft tone. 'A long, long holiday. Somewhere far away.'

'You sound like a GP trying to get rid of an irritating neurotic patient. I am *not* a psychopath,' he said stoutly.

'I'm speaking as your loving wife, not your loving therapist. The Seychelles,' she suggested. 'They're wonderful, I believe.'

'We couldn't possibly go to the Seychelles. We haven't anything like the money, after all we've spent on the house.'

'Perhaps your private practice will perk up?'

'Perhaps,' he said gloomily.

She squeezed his hands. 'Come to bed.'

'I haven't had my dinner yet,' he objected.

'Oh, yes. I was forgetting.'

8

HUGO'S DISQUIET AT the perfection of Marigold's performance vanished from his mind overnight. The midday tour that Friday was a huge success. At the towering, glassy offices of his friend, the stockbroker, just round the corner from St Swithin's in Poultry, the senior stockbrokers signed the petition to Save St Swithin's, the junior ones cheered and clapped and stuffed notes into the collecting-tins.

Marigold's picture had appeared in most of the morning papers, with some caption like 'Florence Nightingale Relights Her Lamp'. This incited two dozen reporters and photographers to gather outside the stockbrokers' offices, with a couple of television crews. Pressed to speak into a tape-recorder, or to face a TV camera, she repeated the same message:

St Swithin's must continue to exist, adding more years to those eight hundred that it has existed already, so beneficially for the people of London. The demands of health are infinite, and they are unpredictable, like the demands of war. With both, I assure you, the planning must be intelligent and determined, to bring success. I yearn to organize our National Health Service, as I organized my hospital in Scutari. At present, unfortunately, the NHS seems to be reorganized weekly, according to whatever complaints happen to appear in the newspapers. Thank you.

Admirable! thought Hugo. Concise, clear, cerebral and controversial.

They crossed the road towards the Bank of England in Threadneedle Street, the procession colourful with red-and-white placards and thrustful with collecting-tins. They penetrated the tiny, twisting City streets off Houndsditch, where a director of an international bank was astutely welcoming such respectable, reliable and costless publicity.

'Marigold, can I take you to lunch?' Hugo invited gratefully. 'I know a sound place opposite the Smithfield meat market.'

She smoothed her long skirt and smiled. 'Dressed like this, they'd probably offer me *baklava* and *raki*.'

'What's that?'

'*Baklava* is a Turkish dish, flaky pasty filled with nuts and honey, much prized in Constantinople. *Raki* is the local fire-water, worse than the Russians' vodka. Our officers and men drank far too much of it, during the war. The Crimean war, of course. You're very kind, but I'd rather go home.'

'Our revels now are ended?' concluded Hugo, who had played Prospero two years ago. 'I cannot thank you enough, Marigold.'

'I assure you that I found it all fascinating and gratifying.'

'Would you mind hanging on to the costume for a bit? St Swithin's might invite you to the wards, to cheer up the patients.'

'Of course. It's most authentic. I feel I have been wearing it for years.'

'Oh! About the port—'

'Open a bottle and drink it yourself. The reflection of your pleasure would delight me much more than my drinking it myself. Here's a hansom.' She stopped a taxi. 'I *am* getting into the character, aren't I?' She laughed, and waved the lamp at him out of the window.

A mile to the west, a legal conference was convening in Chancery Lane.

Sophie and Mandy, clutching their babies, eyed the portentous archway of a stout black door in a glowering Victorian building of red brick. Edwin was paying off the taxi. Jim was at work in Quickprice. Sophie wore a Country Casuals brown check suit, Mandy was dressed as she had for their dinner party. Lawyers invoke better clothes than doctors.

'Wilds – that's the one.'

Edwin ran his finger along the overcrowded brass plate on the doorpost. He pushed the huge doorbell. A young Asian man in a smart blue suit admitted them to a large room glittering with glass partitions and desks, full of busy young people with screens. The new offices had been erected, at staggering expense, behind the original Dickensian walls facing Lincoln's Inn, to preserve the national heritage.

The lift took them to a spacious, pressingly contemporary, office on the top floor. It was empty. Mandy and Sophie placed upon the thick beige carpet their two babies, who immediately got up and started trotting about, dummies in mouth, poking the furniture curiously with their fingers.

'Yours started walking yesterday?' said Sophie resignedly. Had Jeremy started to fly, she would have been only faintly surprised.

Mandy nodded.

'Mine started after you'd left on Tuesday evening,' explained Sophie. 'I think something had been going on between them while we were having dinner. When you collected yours, I noticed they were winking at each other.'

'It's this growing up like a beanstalk that gets me,' complained Mandy. 'Scott suddenly started running up and down stairs. I'd left the front door open to get the shopping in, and if I hadn't grabbed the little bugger by the neck, he'd have been in Hackney Marshes.'

'Hadn't you better tell them to sit down again?' said Edwin nervously. 'After all, one of their better mature qualities is obedience.'

They had already sat down.

'So these are our two little plaintiffs?' Tony Wilds greeted the visitors smoothly, shutting the door. 'They look quite delightful babies to me.'

'They also look delightfully identical,' Edwin pointed out.

'I suppose they do, rather,' said Tony discouragingly, drawing back to look at them. 'I'm not much good at babies, you know. We always have a nanny. Do make yourselves at home,' he invited, indicating the crimson leather sofa and armchairs, which comfortably ensconced clients who paid several hundred pounds an hour for his company.

'Haven't seen you and Sophie for ages,' he smiled at Edwin. 'You really must come and dine at our new little place in South Kensington. And you're Mrs Miles? I hope I can resolve your difficulties.'

Tony Wilds sat behind a stylish desk, rubbing his hands. His brown hair and pale skin were as smooth as the fine cotton shirt from Jermyn Street, the silk tie from the Rue de la Paix, and the Italian suit, in which he slipped along the churning golden conduits of litigation.

'Nice place you got here,' said Mandy.

It is valuable gift, in a world polished with pretentious-ness and illuminated by advertising, to be unimpressed with anything.

She remarked, 'From the outside, I thought I'd be saying hello to Dodson and Fogg.'

'Who?' asked Edwin.

'Aren't you familiar with Dickens?' Tony Wilds smiled at the Kingstons.

'Bardell against Pickwick,' Mandy enlightened them. 'It

really made me laugh, that did, when I read it at school.' She screwed up her nose. 'Mind, I didn't care much for his other books, *Bleak House* and that, when I got them out of the library. He just lost his sense of fun.'

'We all do, I'm afraid, when we get on in the world.' Tony Wilds sighed smoothly.

The other two stared at her. For the working class to appear better educated than themselves was uncomfortable, if not offensive.

'I only wish I had the time to read books,' Sophie excused herself. 'One is so busy.'

'Let's get to business,' said Edwin. 'Ours is Jeremy and hers is Scott. Surely, Tony, you can't tell the difference between them?'

The solicitor inclined his head, as though choosing between bottles of claret.

'I think I could quite easily, with a little more familiarity.'

'Mine *walked* this very week,' declared Sophie, incredulously. 'Not toddled, but started striding about.'

'Mine too,' said Mandy. 'Next year, I'm putting him in for the London Marathon.'

'Only a year old! It's just crazy, utterly crazy, how advanced they are for their age,' Sophie lamented.

'I'm afraid I'm rather hazy about when children start to do things. I didn't really notice my own developing. I don't suppose I shall, until they're old enough to caddy and ghillie for me. Now, tell me what you're complaining about at St Swithin's?' he invited blandly.

'It started on the second of June, the year before last,' Mandy began crisply. 'Sophie and me both had an op at the St Swithin's infertility clinic. To see why we weren't having babies. However hard we were trying to. Didn't we, Sophie?'

'I suppose so,' she agreed uncertainly.

'Would you believe it, the next thing we knew, we'd got a bun in the oven, as my mother used to say.'

'Or, "in the pudding club", I understand?' The solicitor smiled knowledgeably.

'That's right. We both had our babies the same day in April, no trouble at all.'

'So Edwin told me on the telephone.' The solicitor nodded towards him, feeling he should be brought into the maternal consultation.

'We took them home, and soon everyone was saying they didn't look like us, or our husbands, or anyone. Right, Sophie?'

Edwin answered for her. 'Basically.'

He was irritated at Mandy's taking the lead. The more so, for his letting her get away with it.

'So you're saying you were both given the wrong babies?' asked Tony Wilds.

'That's right.' Mandy nodded emphatically.

'The hospital deny it?'

'They would, wouldn't they?'

'But no other mothers, who were there at the time, have complained? I mean, complained about being given the two real babies which you, and Mrs Kingston, actually produced?'

'I suppose not,' Mandy had to agree. 'Perhaps they haven't noticed yet.'

'These babies otherwise are perfectly normal? Apart from being a little advanced in development, which I should have imagined a desirable characteristic. Less time to spend on coddling and caring, less money to spend on baby-sitting when they are precociously older. They seem absolutely splendid little samples of humanity to me,' the solicitor concluded, smiling at them.

'That's the trouble,' Mandy told him. 'They're a bloody sight too perfect.'

'I would hardly have found perfection a matter for complaint,' he suggested sleekly.

'It's spooky. Gives you the shivers. Don't you get me? You don't expect a baby to start marching about like a guardsman, at one year old.'

'Some babies might, surely?' he persisted.

'She's right, they're weird,' Sophie broke in, staring at her son. 'I don't know what it is, but they're not normal.'

'Oh, come!' The solicitor smoothly rubbed his hands. 'Perhaps you're just imagining it? It's very easy to get an *idée fixe* about someone, you know.'

'Mine sometimes makes me think of those films you see on the telly about outer space,' Mandy observed darkly.

'What, you've mothered two little aliens?' the solicitor asked lightly.

'They are *not* human,' Edwin interrupted forcefully. 'And that's the long and the short of it.'

'Oh, come, come, come! You can hardly expect a judge and jury to decide that any two such obvious humans, as those sitting on the carpet, are not.'

'Well, then, what are we going to do to obtain justice?' Edwin asked crossly.

'I don't see any necessity to do anything. I don't see anyone suffering. If the hospital say they are your babies, and nobody else has claimed them over a year, then they must be. No legal action can change that. If they are peculiar babies, I suspect that Napoleon, Einstein, Shakespeare and Plato were all thought distressingly odd by their parents.'

'Are you trying to tell us we've no case?' said Edwin.

'I am afraid you haven't. Take them home and nurture them and love them, and when they grow up you will be enormously proud of them. That is my advice to you. Indeed, it is impossible for me to give you any other.'

They all looked down. The babies were squirming and holding their rounded bellies and making gurgling sounds. Scott pulled his dummy from his mouth and threw it across the room.

'Funny man,' he said, standing up.

'Funny man,' agreed Jeremy, tossing his dummy away, standing up and clasping Scott round the shoulders.

'You think *we're* funny, don't you?' giggled Scott to the company.

'We're friends,' said Jeremy.

'We think you're all silly.'

'We know what's going on. Don't we, Scott?'

'We weren't born yesterday,' said Jeremy.

They clutched each other, choking with laughter.

'My mummy calls your mummy a working-class slut.'

'Oh, thank you,' said Mandy.

'And my mummy calls your mummy a pain in the arse.'

Sophie made no comment.

'We want to go home,' complained Jeremy. 'We're hungry.'

'And thirsty. Can't you fetch us up some milk?'

'Gin and tonic, gin and tonic, I'm dying for a gin and tonic, that's what my mummy's always saying.'

'Shut up!' shouted Sophie. 'Both of you horrible little bastards.'

'I say, steady on,' murmured Edwin.

There was silence.

'Perhaps you have got some sort of case,' Tony Wilds decided. 'Indeed, I think you should see counsel. I suggest Anthony Carver. He's a QC, and an expert in the Family Division.'

'I'm fed up with all this,' said Mandy, rising. 'Can I use your phone?'

'By all means.'

Mandy opened the handbag from Lanzarote, took out a torn piece of newspaper, and dialled a number.

'That *Sunday Morning*? I want to talk to someone. Anyone,' she responded. 'I've got something for you.'

The three adults, and the two children, stared in silence.

'Who? News desk? Right. You ran a story last Sunday about a pair of mixed-up babies. OK? Me and my friend have got a better one. We've got two pair of mixed-up babies. And that's only for a start. Where did it happen? St Swithin's, the hospital they're trying to save, though God knows why. I can talk about it any time you like. Day or night. I'll give you my phone number.' She recited it. 'I'll be home in half an hour.'

She replaced the phone and looked round.

'Leave all this to me,' she assured them.

Shortly after five that evening, Hugo in his white coat slipped into the day-room off Virtue Ward in St Swithin's. This was a small apartment containing half-a-dozen mobile patients watching Gigantic TV News. After the momentous news of the day had been momentously unrolled by Mike, the nationally famous presenter, Mike announced in a jolly way: 'Florence Nightingale died in 1910, and is buried in a country churchyard in Hampshire. But here she is again, come to support the famous St Swithin's Hospital in London, now threatened with closure by government plans for the Health Service.'

Perched on a small table in the corner, Hugo watched her clip with refreshed admiration.

'That's what I like, straight from the shoulder,' said an elderly man in an ancient braided dressing-gown, upon whom Hugo had performed a laparotomy.

'She was in the war, wannshe?' said a sixteen year old

in for kidney examination.

'She used to be on a twenty pound note,' said an appendicectomy.

'Never had a twenty pound note,' said a cholecystectomy.

Hugo slipped away, unnoticed. At seven, Hugo was meeting Alice in the consultants' car park. They usually went home separately, one taking the suburban train from London Bridge – the terminus, Hugo remembered, where Florence Nightingale and her nurses had left for the Crimean war. But today Alice was working late, and he had a report to write up in his office in the Dickens surgical building. About 6.30, his bleep went. He picked up the phone, and was transferred to the porter in his lodge.

'Mr Spratt? There's a lady come to see Miss Nightingale.'

'What sort of lady?'

'She's got a chauffeur-driven car.'

'Can't you get rid of her?'

'She says it's very important, sir. I called you up, because you seem to be Miss Nightingale's spin-doctor.'

'Oh, all right.'

Hugo locked his office and crossed the courtyard to the great gate. He found a thirtyish blonde, smart in black trousers and a black jersey with 'GTV' in gold on on the left shoulder, and carrying a clip-board.

She smiled. 'I'm dreadfully sorry, you must be incredibly busy, but I've just got to see Florence Nightingale. Is she about, anywhere?'

'She's nothing to do with the hospital, you know,' Hugo

told her severely. 'She's just an act we brought in for our "Save St Swithin's" campaign. She's gone home.'

'Can you possibly contact her?' she implored.

'Why?'

'As you see,' she said, picking at her jersey, 'I'm from Gigantic TV.'

Hugo had not seen.

'Our chairman, Richard Crow, was tremendously impressed with her appearance on the five o'clock news programme. He has an interest in your hospital; he's an old friend of a specialist here, Professor Whapshott.'

'Ah, Whapshott,' murmured Hugo.

'Dickie Crow wants Florence Nightingale to appear on the Steve Swift show on Monday.'

Hugo jumped. 'You mean, Sir Stephen Swift? "Sweet and Swift"?'

The visitor nodded.

'In that case – well, I'll see if she's at home.'

To be interviewed by Stephen Swift, Hugo appreciated, was like making confession to the pope.

He took the porter's outside phone. She answered at once.

'Marigold, you were terrific on TV this evening,' he congratulated her warmly.

'Was I? I didn't see. I haven't a television set.'

'Really? How strong-minded. Then perhaps this won't excite you,' he said, less chirpily. 'A TV company want you on their top interview show next Monday. It's called "Sweet and Swift", if that means anything.'

'I should love to,' she said at once.

'Really?' he exclaimed. 'I'm so glad, Marigold. You can give another puff for St Swithin's. Half the nation watches it. They find out by the amount of water flushed down the national loos afterwards.'

He passed the phone to the Gigantic TV emissary, who expressed her delight, said the show was at eight, would she be at the Kennington studios by seven for a run-through and make-up, and they would send a car.

She replaced the phone. 'Florence Nightingale says she'd prefer to make her own way to the studios,' she told Hugo.

'She's very independent.'

The TV lady paused, puzzled. 'You called her Marigold?'

'That's her name.'

'Oh, yes, of course. . . .'

Hugo told Alice about about the invitation as they met in the consultants' car park, a converted cellar under the pathology block, which the consultants' thought pricey.

'It sounds very exciting,' said Alice.

'We can watch it together on Monday night.'

'Darling, I've a meeting on Monday night. How did your morning go?'

'Oh, that was brilliant! Did you see the shot on the evening TV news?'

'Dearest, I've been overwhelmed with patients all day. I'd hardly time for coffee.'

Hugo drove the black Mercedes up the slope, to the St Swithin's back entrance. He always used to ask her, after a day's work, if she had seen anything interesting. But he had decided that in psychiatry there was nothing interesting.

9

A T NOON THE next day, Sophie in her Land Rover, with its bars to ward off stray cattle, drove Mandy and the two infants into the car park of *Sunday Morning*'s office, east of the City of London at Canary Wharf, looking south across the leisurely commerce of the modern Thames.

Edwin had stayed at home, protesting that he, understandably, had work to catch up. He had become confused, disgusted and nauseated with the whole arduous affair. It was clearly another of life's misfortunes, to be stoically borne, like illness or bankruptcy. It was inexplicable, it was beyond disentanglement, but, with luck, it might later be found to merit less excitement than everyone was now extravagantly lavishing upon it. Jim had a ticket for West Ham v. Arsenal.

Being Saturday, *Sunday Morning* was going to bed, worthily furthering democracy, and fearlessly exhibiting the freedom of the Press, by whirring out five million copies of scandalous and salacious secrets impartially of the high and low, the high being far the more preferable.

When Mandy had phoned from Chancery Lane the

previous afternoon, Paula Smith was tapping her keyboard sitting opposite the news editor, in the large, crowded room, atwinkle with screens and abuzz with phones, in which *Sunday Morning* was concocted.

'Paula – you know about St Swithin's Hospital, don't you?' asked the news editor.

'Yes, I'm doing a piece on one of the professors.' She indicated her screen.

'Someone there's mixed up some babies. Might be worth looking into. St Swithin's is getting plenty of cover at the moment, now they've reincarnated Florence Nightingale. Would you like to take a smell at the story?' He tossed Mandy's phone number across the desk. 'She'll be there in half an hour.'

'If you like,' Paula agreed. 'I'm seeing the learned professor again on Friday. Though I don't think mixed-up babies are quite his line.'

Paula introduced herself on the telephone, and Mandy tumbled out her story.

'Look, I'd like a chat about this business,' Paula decided. 'Could you two mothers come and have lunch tomorrow at our office? Bringing the babies, of course. We have infant feeding facilities.'

'They're eating fish and chips,' said Mandy.

The mothers and babies were escorted to an upper room with wicker furniture and a jungle of potted plants. Paula was waiting. Unlike their solicitor, she saw instantly both the startling likeness, and the grotesque maturity, of the two offspring. The babies were set in two wicker armchairs, sucking dummies.

'When did it all start?' Paula began, in her pragmatic way.

'Well, it was last Monday morning when we told St Swithin's about it,' said Sophie.

'Why, I was in St Swithin's last Monday morning! Quite a coincidence. I was interviewing Professor Whapshott.'

'Whapshott? But that's the doctor we're seeing about it next Friday. Isn't it, Mandy?'

'That's right. Whapshott. Funny name.'

'When he gets back from America,' Sophie elaborated. 'He's having a tour.'

'Why are you seeing Professor Whapshott? He's nothing to do with midwives and nappies and such?'

'They think it might be due to our genes, or something,' said Mandy.

'Really?' murmured Paula. 'That's interesting.'

'The genes bit is beyond me,' confessed Mandy. 'I've heard about genes, who hasn't, like I've heard about hypnotists, but I don't see how either of them can make us do things we don't want to.'

Paula switched on the tape recoder on the wickerwork table.

'Do you mind if I put you on tape? Now, reveal to me absolutely everything that happened. Right from the beginning.'

They recounted their obstetrical history, at which they were now more practised than Hugo with Hamlet.

A penny beyond price dropped in Paula's head.

'Tell me,' she invited. 'When you were in St Swithin's, were you ever bitten by mosquitoes?'

'Funny you should say that,' exclaimed Mandy. 'We was, wasn't we, Sophie? When we were at that infertility clinic, what we just told you about.'

'Did you tell the St Swithin's doctors about this, last Monday?'

'Yes, we did.'

'What did they say?'

'They didn't take any notice.'

'Some mosquitoes!' recalled Sophie. 'Why, it was like being bitten by a vampire.'

'Mine was this size.' Mandy spread finger and thumb three inches apart. 'They ought to have been in a zoo.'

'You were both bitten? By outsize mosquitoes? On the same day? Then you both became pregnant?'

The pair nodded.

'What happened to the mosquitoes?'

'We killed 'em,' said Mandy. 'A proper danger, they were.'

'I hate buzzing things,' said Sophie.

Paula removed the tape from her recorder, rummaged in her briefcase, and inserted another.

Scott took his dummy from his mouth.

'Wanna piss.'

'We've changing facilities downstairs,' said Paula calmly.

'He can use the loo,' said Mandy disconsolately. 'He was caught short during my late shopping in Quickprice yesterday.'

'Second on the right outside,' directed Paula.

Mandy opened the door, then the door in the corridor with the male silhouette, and waited outside.

The financial correspondent of *Sunday Morning*, a tall thin man in a dark suit with a handkerchief in the pocket, who wrote a short column telling readers how to make easy money on the Stock Exchange, was occupying one of two urinals thinking about the trend in bond yields. He glanced idly to one side, to see a one-year-old child in a hat with a blue bobble and sucking a dummy, standing peeing powerfully against the porcelain.

The financial correspondent terminated his activity, rapidly adjusted his dress, and staggered into the news room.

'In the gents,' he gasped to the fashion editor, a hatchet-faced Londoner wearing a sari. 'I've just seen something peculiar. A small child standing up and peeing.'

'They mature early these days,' she mentioned.

'But not as early as this. I must have been seeing things. He was sucking a dummy. I must sit down.' He took a sheet of her copy and fanned himself.

'Is the medical correspondent in the room?' she asked, looking round.

'The child might have been driving a car, or using a cash-point. It was a shock. I must have a drink,' he decided, rising and making for the door. 'If I want to go again, I shall wait until I get home.'

'Listen to this,' said Paula, when Mandy and Scott returned among the potted plants.

She switched on the recorder:

I'll tell you exactly what I do, my life's work. But until it's perfected, I don't want it published.

Off the record.

I create perfect human beings, who live for ever.

Go on?

Jiang, bring a specimen of Adam and Eve.

Silence, then an intense buzzing.

But those mosquitoes are huge!

Size is the least of their unique qualities. The mosquitoes contain carefully modified genes. They would create a man, or a woman, free from suffering any known disease. . . .

Paula switched off.

Sophie and Mandy were leaning forward, listening open-mouthed. Jeremy and Scott had gone to asleep.

'There's more,' Paula instructed them. 'That was Professor Whapshott.'

'Who we're going to see,' nodded Sophie.

'Exactly. It's all coming together. Listen carefully, please. These mosquitoes were loaded with the genes for producing perfect human beings. All of them identical human beings. You're with me?'

They nodded again.

'But the professor has a problem. If these mosquitoes mate, they breed only more mosquitoes. They obviously have the usual mosquito genes on board, as well. To get his designer genes into a human female, to produce a perfect human baby, seemed to Professor Whapshott impossible. If a human female went to bed with a mosquito, it simply wouldn't work.'

'Painful, too,' said Mandy.

'So Professor Whapshott's life's work, for which he was expecting to win the Nobel Prize, had come to nothing. He is performing numerous experiments to transfer his genes into human shape. You seem to have done it for him.'

The two mothers stared at each other. Sophie had gone pale.

'But how?' she asked.

'By getting bitten by his king-size mosquitoes. A pair escaped. A bite was enough. It had not occurred to the professor that such erudite problems could have such simple solutions. It's always happening with these learned scientists. I expect that Newton thought up gravity, but wondered what it did exactly until the apple bonked him on the head,' said Paula, with journalistic license.

'I thought mosquito bites gave you malaria,' said Sophie.

'These ones give you pregnancy.'

'Then what do we do?' asked Sophie despairingly.

'Make a lot of money,' said Mandy.

'Oh, we'll pay you all right,' Paula assured her readily.

'This is going to be the story of the year.'

'Of the century!' Mandy corrected her forcefully. 'We'll want millions.'

'Millions?' responded Paula. 'Well, that's perhaps rather a lot.'

'Is it? I wouldn't know. I never discuss money,' said Mandy. 'You'll have to see Terry Boxer.'

'Terry Boxer!' exclaimed Paula.

'Terry Boxer,' said Mandy with satisfaction.

'You don't mean Terry Boxer?' asked Sophie.

Terry Boxer was famed, Terry Boxer was feared, throughout the Western world. He was a publicist, who effortlessly generated his publicity. Some are born famous, some achieve fame, and some have fame thrust upon them; and Terry Boxer brilliantly handled the errors and eccentricities of all three. Errant duchesses, wild pop stars, sexually aberrant politicians, swindling financiers and spectacular murderers, all came to him with the hope and the gratitude of the sick to their doctor, and got more reliable satisfaction.

'You've been on to Terry already?' Paula asked unbelievingly.

'I rang his office yesterday afternoon and told them the tale. He's in New York, but he's back next week. They gave him a call, and he promised to take us on.'

'That was very shrewd of you,' Paula conceded.

'You never told me,' complained Sophie mildly.

'Sorry, luv. I was keeping it as a little surprise. I mean, *Sunday Morning* might have told us to go and get stuffed.'

'I think you're wonderful,' said Sophie absently.

'Mind, this deal will be for newspaper rights only,' Mandy told Paula. 'TV and that will be separate.'

'I'll have to agree with that,' said Paula. 'Terry will see to it.'

'Are we *really* going to make all this money from the newspapers?' Sophie added dreamily.

'For a start. Whatever your smart-arsed lawyer said, St Swithin's are in this up to their haircuts. I can't wait to have a little chat with that Sir whatever he is.'

'If I may say so, Mandy, I admire the way you're handling this catastrophe,' Paula complimented her.

'I got it from my dad. He worked in a betting-shop, and he was sharper than a bag of tacks. He had to be. It's all in my genes.' She laughed loudly. 'What odds will you lay on my genes? Hundred to one on, I'd say.'

'I wanna go home,' said Scott.

'Where's my lunch?' said Jeremy.

The mothers turned. They had forgotten them.

When they left later in the Land Rover, Sophie kissed Mandy. There is no snobbery, there is no class distinction, among millionaires.

On Sunday, Hugo and Alice had lunch with his parents in Richmond.

'I suppose that new drug's doing me good?' asked his father gloomily, as they sat at the long bare dining-table in his riverside mansion.

Peregrine Lancelot Spratt was skinnier and vaguer than his surgical father. He was bald and unbearded and wore

THE LAST OF SIR LANCELOT ·

thick-framed glasses. He was dressed in brown tweed trousers, a bright red shirt and a canary cashmere pullover. His literary contribution to the world's ambience had brought him more of cultured appreciation than cash, but Sir Lancelot had left him well-off, and his inheritance well-advised, from post-operative chats with the financial experts in the City who regularly fell under his knife. When Sir Lancelot's will was published, there were jealous opinions in St Swithin's that he could never have earned that much with his surgery.

'Which drug?' asked Hugo.

His father was on uncountable drugs, some prescribed by his GP, some by Hugo himself, and the bulk bought over the local chemists' counters. Their Sunday lunches were mostly consultations with catering.

'That one I was prescribed with the funny name. Sumo. Why should anyone want to call a drug that?'

'It's made by a big Japanese firm, Dad. Placenta Pharmaceuticals. I suppose they thought it was a smart name, with an easily remembered local connection.'

'Oh, those grotesque wrestlers? The only Japanese the English know, along with Shogun cars and The Mikado jolly songs. Everyone I speak to seems to be on Sumo.'

'It's Placenta's top drug. It revitalizes the myocardium, you know, so you get no cardiac diseases. Much.'

'There's a report due out about it soon,' added Alice informatively. 'There's been a vast survey in Europe and America. Of the patients who are prescribed it.'

'Nobody asked me,' said Peregrine, more gloomily.

'Cicely!' called his mother, sitting across the table.

Fran Francis was a blonde brighter than ever, still glorious, if conspicuously fatter than the breathtaking teenaged actress who played in a revival of *Private Lives* after World War Two. She was costumed in a floor-length knitted crimson dress, flapping with black lace. She was reading *The Stage* beside her plate. She always used a lorgnette.

'Yes, Fran?'

They employed the young cordon bleu cook in a green overall for Sunday lunch. The rest of the week they ate instant food from the freezer, whenever they were not dining at restaurants of varying extravagance.

'What am I supposed to be eating?'

'*Feuilleté d'asperges*. I'm giving you a spring lunch.'

'*Feuilleté d'asperges*?' said Fran, in the tone of Lady Bracknell mentioning handbags. 'I had *feuilleté d'asperges* far better than this in the Caprice in 1960.'

'I'm sure you did, Fran.' Cicely was adjusting the hot plate on the sideboard.

'And in that restaurant in Paris – what was it, Pery?'

'The Grand Vefour, dear.'

'Of course! Dear Georges was the *maître d'hôtel*.'

Fran plunged her suspended fork in the asparagus. Cicely smiled. How wonderful, to play scenes with Fran Francis!

'Jimmy's putting on a revival of *Hay Fever*,' Fran observed, reading between mouthfuls. 'On the pier at Brighton. Oh, dear.'

'Aren't piers good business?' asked Hugo. 'People have nowhere else to go on wet nights.'

'Brighton is very bracing, I suppose,' she admitted.

'Did you read my novel?' Peregrine asked Alice.

'I read reviews of it.'

'That's what everyone says,' he complained crossly. 'Which ones?'

'Well, in the *Sunday Times*.'

'That man's an imbecile. Complete idiot! Doesn't even begin to understand my work. A contemptible review.'

'Blinkie's opening a new musical at the Shaftesbury,' observed Fran, cleaning her plate. 'Risky, musicals, these days. It's about rustic life. Might appeal. Could put something in it.' She was a theatrical angel, with a level halo. 'What's this?' she demanded, as Cicely reappeared.

'*Côtes d'agneau de lait et son paté.*'

'I had that in Monte Carlo in 1970. What was the name of that wonderful chef?'

'Gascard Gautier,' said Peregrine.

'That's right!'

'What should I do about my diet?' Peregrine asked his son.

'Well, avoid fatty meat. Don't eat hamburgers.'

'Hamburgers?' He looked shocked. 'Who on earth would eat a hamburger? My stomach has not been at all well, recently. Not at all. It feels quite serious.'

'I'll have a look at you upstairs after lunch,' said Hugo dutifully.

Many Sunday afternoons included his father lying on the

four-poster bed while he palpated his abdomen.

'Your father is a dreadful hypochondriac,' said Sir Lancelot, who was sitting opposite. 'Full of useless medicines. But I suppose if you stopped them, it would kill him.'

'Are you addressing me, or the family?' Hugo speculated.

'Oh, the others aren't aware of me. The grub looks good.'

Sir Lancelot took a pinch of snuff. He wore his black jacket and striped trousers, he glowed discretely, and Hugo could see Cicely at the sideboard through him.

'I wanted a word, dear boy, about the Health Minister. What's his name? Goodie. The vandal who's avid to close St Swithin's down.'

'I've never met him. He only talks to doctors about reducing our pay.'

'He goes on about waiting-lists. In my view, they're a sign of success. You never get a queue outside a dud show. Ask your mother.'

'I suppose killing off half our patients would solve the problem,' Hugo speculated thoughtfully.

'Trouble is, dear boy, medicine's too efficient. The more efficient we are, the more money we need. Like the army or the fire brigade. Florrie's been going on about this, hasn't she? Pity she can't shine her lamp on the Health Minister. Why not get them together?'

'Impossible, Grandad. Bert Goodie's surrounded by Civil Service bouncers. He doesn't see much point in outside opinions, when he has plenty of opinions of his own.'

'Pity. A bossy woman like Florrie would get the Health

Service pulling together like a Boat Race crew. What happened about those two abnormal infants you were telling me about?'

'It all seems to have blown over.'

'Perhaps I was being rather spooky. Probably nothing in it. These scares come and go. Do you remember the story of Mary Toft? She gave birth to seventeen rabbits in 1726. Ended up in Bridewell prison, poor thing. Well, I must be going. This is the last time we shall meet, dear boy, until – well, we won't go into that.'

'Oh, no!' cried Hugo in disappointment. His grandfather's wraith, he decided, was the most pleasant member of the family.

'I've enjoyed our chats. But I can't remain down here any longer. It's not at all done. Particularly as I'll want an exeat for Lord's at the Test.'

He vanished.

'I'm sorry,' Hugo apologized hastily. 'My attention wandered off for a minute or two.'

'It didn't at all,' his mother contradicted him. 'I was about to ask what show you were doing at the hospital?'

Hugo told her.

'Not like that!' she objected. 'You can't play Hamlet in a beard, no more than you can play Father Christmas without one.'

Hugo stroked it, as fondly as a pet pup condemned to be put down.

'I always wanted to play Ophelia,' she reflected. 'But no one ever asked me.'

'After lunch, I'll read you my two new poems,' Peregrine announced.

'On a nice day like this, after lunch we're going for a walk in Richmond Park,' Fran corrected him. 'Where did your Florence Nightingale come from?' she enquired from Hugo. 'Has she been in rep? Doing TV?'

'She's an amateur player,' said Hugo. 'Like me.'

'Really? You should send her to RADA. She'd be another Gertrude Lawrence.'

Fran had little regard for Nöel Coward's favourite actress.

In the Mercedes driving home, Hugo said at once, 'I saw Sir Lancelot again. When we were having the lamb. Did you notice?'

Alice shook her head. 'Nobody noticed anything. You were talking to your dad about his multiple diseases.'

'It's so odd. I had a five-minute conversation with Grandpa. He was sitting across the table, wearing his formal gear and sniffing snuff, as I well remember he used to.'

'And what did he say, darling?' Alice asked softly.

'That I should get Florence Nightingale to meet Bert Goodie, our Health Minister.'

Alice gently laid her fingers on his hand, attached to the steering wheel.

'Hugo, you *are* having these illusions quite severely, aren't you?'

'But she's not an illusion! How can she be? The whole country's seen her in the morning papers and on television.'

'Yes, yes,' said Alice comfortingly. 'The whole country's

seen an amateur actress called—?'

'Marigold Peacock.'

'Playing Florence Nightingale on TV, as your mother said. And the whole country believes they're really seeing Florence Nightingale, because they want to.'

'Like the Loch Ness Monster?' he recalled. 'Or strange objects flying in the sky. Or people from outer space.'

'What's wrong with that? These visions don't do any of us any harm.'

'I suppose they provide a pleasant interest to people with dull lives. Which is most people.'

'I agree, dearest,' she continued patiently. 'But I'm worried about Florence Nightingale and you.'

'You're jealous of her?'

'No more than I am jealous of the ghost of Anne Boleyn in the Tower of London.'

'With her head tucked underneath her arm.'

'But I am concerned, that you have become so deluded, that you treat this female, and talk about her, as though she was the real Florence Nightingale on leave from the Crimean War.'

'Do I?' Hugo looked astounded.

'Patients with severe illusions are often unaware of the clinical picture they present. Or perhaps reluctant to admit it to themselves.'

'That's a load of balls,' said Hugo crossly.

'Darling!'

'Florence Nightingale behaves like Florence Nightingale, so I treat her like Florence Nightingale. When my mother was on tour as Cleopatra, the staff in all the hotels treated her like Cleopatra.'

'They would have no choice.'

'I am not in the slightest schizophrenic, paranoiac, psycho-somatic or neurotic. I am a perfectly normal hard-working consultant surgeon, who is trying to build up a private practice so that we can raise a family to romp about in Dulwich.'

'Hugo, dear, why don't you see Gus?'

'Gus!' He sounded the horn loudly at an old lady who was walking in the middle of the road on a pedestrian crossing. 'I hate bloody Gus.'

'He's a terribly good psychiatrist. He could do you a lot of good.'

'If you imagine I'm going to lie down on a couch and reveal my innermost secrets to a solemn shrink like Gus, you're wrong.'

'Dear one,' she cooed. 'I do wish you wouldn't call us "shrinks". I hope you've revealed your innermost secrets to me?'

'All of them. And I hope you to me,' he said briskly.

'Except one.'

'Oh?' He turned his eyes from the road, looking concerned. 'What's that? You're having an affair with Gus?'

'I'm pregnant.'

'What!'

He blew the horn again, at some car objecting to his jumping a red light.

'Why didn't you tell me before?' he asked in confusion.

'I found out only yesterday, when I said I had to go to the hospital. I had an appointment with Sir Clarence in the Nightingale building. I'd done the test myself, of course, but I wanted to get everything definite. I didn't tell you about it, because you've been in such a peculiar psychological state these last few days. I didn't know what the effect would be. You might go manic, and start tearing down the curtains. I decided to wait until you'd got over the stress of having Sunday lunch with your parents, and reveal it when you were lying relaxed in bed tonight. I'm due in January.'

'Darling, darling, darling Alice!'

'It's wonderful, isn't it ? Sweet, delicious, lovely Hugo!'

They kissed passionately.

'What are you stopping for?' she asked, puzzled.

'You didn't notice the blue lights in the mirror?'

10

AT EIGHT O'CLOCK on Monday evening, Hugo reclined alone in his Dulwich living-room in an easy chair, his hands clasped across his stomach and his feet on the coffee-table, at his left elbow a white plastic dish of eaten instant shepherd's pie, at his right a half-empty bottle of '95 Pommard, and watching television.

'And now – Steve Swift!'

Fanfare. Roll of drums.

'Good evening.'

Steve Swift was silver-haired, in a silver suit with a silver bow-tie. He sat at a plain table with glasses of water.

'My first guest tonight is a national heroine. No voice in the country could be raised against that. She brilliantly organized the care of our wounded soldiers, in the most disastrously conducted war in our history. More than that, she founded hospital nursing, as we know it today. When ever – where ever – you receive the skilled care of a nurse, you owe it to – the Lady with the Lamp, Florence Nightingale!'

Fanfare. Roll of drums.

Sweeping her skirt, Florence sat opposite in her lace cap.

'Good evening, Miss Nightingale. You said last week that you longed to reorganize the National Health Service. How would you start?'

'By removing it from political control.'

'But Miss Nightingale! You must admit that is impossible?'

'I am glad of your emphatic contradiction, Sir Stephen,' said Florence quietly. 'It affirms the difficulty of my task. But it can be done. It must be done. The supreme authority on health matters should be a body of reputable experts, enjoying complete independence from the government. There is a convenient example: our supreme authority on financial matters is the Bank of England, which is now totally independent. Surely the nation's health is more valuable than the nation's wealth?'

Loud applause.

'You mention the Bank of England. But surely the government must control the fifty billion or so of taxpayers' money which the NHS needs yearly?'

'That very power is attractive to politicians. So is the intimate nature of the National Health Service, reaching into the body of every citizen, present at every sickness, at every childbearing, and at every death. What prime minister in my day – Palmerston, Disraeli, Gladstone – could have imagined wielding such influence over the voters? The Health Service has become nothing but a bribe during elections, and a political Punch and Judy show in between. I have come to believe that politicians are not seriously interested in health, except their own.'

Loud applause.

'But your independent health authority, which I would compare to the BBC—'

'I'd prefer you to compare it with the Established Church.'

'. . . will still have to raise a lot of money. How would you do it?'

'People detest paying taxes. They stampede to bet. The National Lottery should contribute to the National Health. The lottery raises some five billion pounds a year. It would help. It would pay the drugs bill.'

'But Miss Nightingale! What about the arts?'

'The arts can look after themselves. It is no use being cultured if you are dead.'

Applause.

'Then how would you raise the rest of the money?'

'Taxes, obviously. But they should be earmarked for health. Like the Road Fund was earmarked for roads. Until it was raided by Lloyd George, of course. This money must be spent with prudence, not on pet schemes for either ambitious doctors or self-seeking politicians. Do you know the British Ambassador in Constantinople wished to dispense the entire thirty thousand pounds raised by *The Times*, on a Protestant church in sight of the Golden Horn? Fortunately, I was able to dissuade him, and spent the money on knives and forks, soap and towels, food and drink, bedding and clothing. You were nursed in what you were wounded in.'

'When you were in the Crimea—'

'I was not in Crimea. I was at Scutari.'

'One of your patients wrote this.' Steve Swift picked up a script. ' "What a comfort it was to see her pass, even. She would speak to one and nod and smile to as many more, but she could not do it to all, you know. We lay there in hundreds, we could but kiss her shadow as it fell, we lay our heads on the pillow again, content". You had a wonderfully merciful effect on the sufferers, we all agree.'

Loud applause.

'But would *that* enable you to manage the multiple complications of our modern Health Service?'

'I first entered my wards to discover they were four miles of corridors with patients lying on the floors. The daily death rate was forty-five. We had two hundred and fifty soldiers' wives and widows in the basements, getting drunk and prostituting themselves. The orderlies had chopped up the operating tables for firewood. I needed to overcome many awkward problems, and many awkward personalities, to improve matters. I started by nursing the British Army, I ended by feeding it, clothing it, writing its letters home, and burying a good proportion of it. I am proud of that. And I am proud of our Health Service. It was the very first in the world. It deserves better from its masters.'

Applause.

'But one woman reorganizing the NHS! You'd need Divine intervention.'

Florence Nightingale suddenly smiled. 'I saw the other day a note I had written to myself: "I *must* remember God is not my private secretary".'

Titters.

'Well, I wish you luck. Have you any message to give, now, about nursing patients?'

'Yes. There is nothing yet discovered which is a substitute to the English patient for his cup of tea. He can take it when he can take nothing else, and often can't take anything else if he has it not. I should be very glad if any of tea's opponents would point out what to give to an English patient after a sleepless night, instead of tea.'

'I raise my cup. A wonderful trip through history. Thank you, Florence Nightingale.'

Loud applause.

Fanfare. Roll of drums.

Hugo toasted her with his glass of Pommard, and finished it off. He folded his fingers again on his abdomen, and for the rest of the programme went to sleep.

He was at St Swithin's early on Tuesday morning. At 8.30, he entered the coffee-room in the theatre suite, wearing his theatre blues, looking for a cup before operating. He found Amanda.

'I've just seen your first case, in the ward,' she greeted him. 'He's got a cardiac arrhythmia.'

'Then he'll have to be seen by a physician.'

'He should have been seen by a physician yesterday. Patients don't like such a catastrophe as an operation being put off. Even Blackbeard the Pirate wouldn't have cared to face walking the plank twice.'

'Do you have to be so offensive?' Last night's Pommard, followed by his grandfather's port, had made him irritable.

'Why, you've shaved it off!'

Hugo fondled his chin. 'It was itching.'

Amanda looked at him critically. 'I think I preferred you with it on.'

The telephone on the table rang.

'This *is* Mr Spratt,' he responded, sipping coffee.

'It's Mr Harvey, from *The Daily Post*,' said the switchboard female. 'All right to put him through?'

'Yes, please do.'

'We're getting an awful lot of calls for Florence Nightingale, Mr Spratt. I tell them that she doesn't work here any more.'

'Oh, put them on to Gigantic TV. They're used to that sort of thing.'

Bill Harvey had written a series for the *Post* about the worldwide disaster of closing St Swithin's, with which Hugo had enthusiastically collaborated. A pleasant fellow, generous with his drinks.

'Hugo? Nice to talk again. Florence Nightingale was brilliant last night,' Bill Harvey began warmly. 'I was fascinated. She's just like the real thing. Probably better. Congratulations! She's made all the papers this morning.'

'They hadn't arrived when I left home.'

'I wanted to get her for a full-page interview. That OK?

Have you got her phone number?'

Hugo gave it. 'If she's not there, try Chiddingford Hall in Kent. Her real name's Marigold Peacock.'

It occurred to Hugo that he had no notion where Marigold lived. She had given him an inner London number, he supposed to the flat where the bailiffs had besieged her husband. He poured some coffee. The door opened to admit Trevor Blewett, in his blues, theatre cap on head, mask round neck.

'Hugo! I've caught you before you scrub-up. I saw your girlfriend on TV last night.' He grinned. 'I feel honoured that you gave us a preview of her performance in the committee-room. It was such a hit that Bert Goodie wants to meet her.'

Hugo looked astonished.

'You heard what she said on the programme?' he emphasized. 'She wants to run the NHS. Which Bert Goodie is paid to do himself. It'll hardly be a meeting of minds.'

'He's dead keen, old man. He rang me at home this morning. He has some great idea for her. I don't know what it is. You know how Bert Goodie gets great ideas.'

'Like stopping people smoking by putting arsenic in every tenth cigarette?'

'I admit that Russian roulette of the lighter idea didn't get far,' Trevor Blewett said grudgingly. 'He's got a drinks party at the Ministry of Health at six tomorrow, and he'd like both of you to come along.'

'I'll see if she can.'

Hugo took an outside line. Marigold answered at once. He extended the Health Minister's invitation.

'I should be delighted to accept. I'm extremely pleased that the Minister himself has decided to meet me. I shall join you outside the Ministry at six o'clock.'

'You know where the ministry is?' Hugo asked helpfully.

'Of course.'

'You'll come in costume, won't you?'

'I should feel strange in anything else.'

Hugo smiled, replacing the phone. 'That's fine. It's funny,' he reflected, 'Sir Lancelot Spratt was urging me to have her meet the Minister of Health.'

Mr Blewett looked confused.

'When did he say that?'

'On Sunday, during lunch.'

'Hugo – er, your distinguished grandfather, though cherished in the minds of all surgeons here, has been pushing up the daisies for pushing on half a century.'

'Oh! Yes, of course. I was forgetting.'

Mr Blewett eyed him like a difficult abdomen.

'Sure you're all right?'

'Perfectly. I was preoccupied by my first patient.'

'How's Alice?'

'Alice! Oh, she's had some good news.' He stopped. Trevor Blewett would not appreciate it. 'She's got bonus points from the supermarket.'

'Do you talk psychiatry to Alice?'

'Every night.'

'Well, you'd better tonight,' suggested Mr Blewett, leaving.

The telephone rang. It was Bill Harvey again.

'I can't get any reply from that number,' he said shortly.

'Really? But I've just spoken to her on it.'

'I tried Chiddingford Hall, but some official told me there was no Florence Nightingale there.'

'That's her stage name—'

'Nor Peacock. The place is a museum of Kentish palaeontology.'

'I've got to go and operate,' said Hugo, impatient of the inconsiderate people that morning surrounding him.

'Ugh,' said Bill Harvey.

At five to six the next evening, Hugo was waiting on the pavement of Belgrave Square, outside the Ministry of Health. At six, Florence arrived in a taxi.

'It's paid, Mr Spratt,' she affirmed amiably, waving him aside.

Hugo vaguely wondered how. She never carried a handbag.

They presented themselves to a row of counters with windows of bullet-proof glass. They were issued with plastic oblongs giving their names, which fascinated Florence. She smiled, attaching hers to the shoulder of her costume.

'Usually, I don't need to be labelled like mutton.'

She seems in lighthearted mood this evening, Hugo thought. Greatly as he admired her demeanour, she sometimes reminded him of the female whom his father had employed when he was six, who, the necessity of eating up greens being outdated in child care, dosed him twice daily with spoonfuls of vitamins.

A tall, beaky man in a grey suit appeared to take them upstairs. In a large panelled room, hung with portraits of former ministers of health, a knot of smart men and women were already chattering intensely. As Florence entered, they turned, smiled and clapped. The Health Minister emerged from the middle.

Herbert Goodie was a short, plump man with restless eyes and a bristly haircut. He was the son of a docker at Blue Water Wharf, which, like himself, had recently been greatly improved. He recognized that he was the bossy type, and thought that the soundest way to rise in the world was not seeking equality, but superiority. He had started work as a park-keeper, enjoyably commanding forgetful strollers to keep off the grass. At the weekend, he refereed local football matches, but was dropped after ending up on a bare pitch after sending off twenty-two players. He decided to be a policeman, but the police did not concur with him. He considered a taxi driver, with the route and the conversation constantly under his power to switch. He became a traffic warden in Greenwich, which afforded him total fulfilment.

One afternoon, he was applying a ticket to a new BMW when the owner appeared, a prosperous-looking middle-aged man.

THE LAST OF SIR LANCELOT ·

'Sorry I'm a minute late. I was caught short on the way out.'

'I've 'eard 'em all,' Bert Goodie assured him.

'You've got a kind face. I'd like to give you a little present.'

'More than my job's worth.'

'I'm collecting rather a lot of these things,' the driver reflected. 'I must get round to paying them sometime. The police are getting nasty. Do you live round here?' he asked, sweeping his hand towards the Naval College.

'If you must know, I lives over the river at Blue Water Wharf. There's your ticket.'

'Thank you. But so do I! Have you thought of joining the local council?'

Bert asked why he should want to join the council.

'It's a wonderful job. Order about anyone you like in the borough. Lavish expenses, too. I could fix it. I'm the mayor.'

Bert took back the ticket. 'Any more of them on you?'

The mayor produced a handful. It was the start of Bert Goodie's career. Now he was in Parliament, among several similar successful men. The only trace of his passage there was an occasional aspirate dropped in his spoor.

He was a man who made up his mind decisively and swiftly, as Florence Nightingale was about to discover.

'Perfect!' He looked her up and down. 'Just what we're looking for. Let's have a talk, before the place gets over-crowded. Come and sit down over 'ere.'

The pair occupied a yellow silken *chaise-longue* under a picture of Nye Bevan. Hugo stood at one end, the man in grey at the other. A white-jacketed steward attended with a bottle of champagne; a waitress in a black dress and white apron held the canapés.

Florence took a glass of champagne.

'The points you made on TV last night,' began Bert Goodie. 'One: that the 'ealth service should be right out of politics. It should be as independent as the Bank of England. I'm with you on that, a hundred per cent.'

She smiled, and took a caviar nibble. 'I am gratified and surprised that you should agree with me, Mr Goodie.'

'I should be the governor, of course,' he mentioned. 'Then I could get on with the job, without being hassled every day by opposition MPs trying to make something out of it. Not to mention, come to think of it, by big-headed pressure-groups. WHAMS!' he exclaimed in disgust. 'What's WHAMS? Anyone heard of WHAMS?'

'It's an organization of pushy medical women,' Hugo told him. 'I don't know what they do. I don't think they know themselves.'

The minister bit into a jumbo prawn. 'It's my job to get a hold on the basics in medicine and surgery. Right? And what happens?'

Florence took another caviar.

'Enoch Powell—' Bert Goodie indicated the portrait. 'I quote him: "The unnerving discovery that every minister of health makes at or near the onset of his term of office is that the only subject he is ever destined to discuss with the medical profession is money". Money! For months I've been telling Ronnie at the Treasury that we want our hands on the Lottery boodle, just like you said on TV. He talks about the National 'eritage. What's that? A load of old ruins. You like opera?'

'I once heard Jenny Lind sing *Der Freischutz.*'

The Minister ignored this. 'I get tapes, and listen to them in the bath. Much cheaper, and you don't have to dress up. Listen—' He leant forward. 'I've got a job for you.'

Florence had her champagne replenished. Living it up a bit today, Hugo reflected.

'It's a big job. But if it works, I'll be shovelling up the Lottery money, and Charlie in Number Ten will have to think very, very carefully about making us independent. Charlie doesn't like any department to get overmighty, and certainly not overloved. He's got to have both, power and pop, or he wouldn't enjoy his cornflakes. Remember that letter, what they read out on your programme? We want the patients to kiss the shadow of the NHS as it falls, then lay their heads on the pillow again, content. The NHS wants a new face. Like – any examples, Harry?' he asked the acolyte beside him.

'Well, Minister, the gas industry sold itself to an imaginary shareholder called Sid. Then there was this funny little man in a bowler and moustache representing the Inland Revenue.'

He ignored them. 'I want the sympathy of the people. I want them marching behind the NHS, like behind the army at war. Just like you said. People then would put up with practically anything, which would save us a lot of bother. Your image is out of this world, and you know it,' he continued realistically. 'You'd be our mouthpiece for ministry statements—'

'Many of which, we must admit, Minister, are becoming somewhat unpleasant for the public to hear,' intervened the acolyte.

'You'd be on our Press releases, you'd be on TV commercials, you'd be on billboards,' Bert Goodie told her triumphantly. 'You'll have to attend medical functions, visit the sick in hospitals and that, but I can do that in my sleep. Just be yourself. I mean, just be the real Florence Nightingale,' he remembered.

'I should be delighted, Mr Goodie.'

'Fine!' He munched a flaky sausage roll. 'We'll release the story tomorrow. You'll need a pic with the prime minister, for the Friday papers. Harry, ring Number Ten and see when Charlie can make it.'

'What about saving St Swithin's?' Hugo ventured.

'Oh, we'll find some excuse to keep it open,' the minister said airily. 'After all, St Swithin's is a grand brand name. Like St Michael and St Ivel.'

'And St Emilion,' nodded Hugo.

'And you can make as many suggestions on running the NHS as you like,' Bert Goodie told Florence generously, tapping her hand.

'Miss Nightingale has already made some, about the apparently inevitable annual winter crisis, to Mr Blewett,' said Hugo.

'You were behind that, were you? I thought it was the most sensible paper the old fart had ever shown me.'

'Eight tomorrow morning, Minister,' said the acolyte, returning.

At quarter to eight on the Thursday morning, Hugo was waiting outside the black metal gates guarding Downing Street. Florence Nightingale arrived in a taxi, raising cries of 'Oo, look!' from passers-by. Policemen took them to No. 10, a gold-braided doorkeeper admitted them, an official received them.

Hugo stared round, awed.

'I've never been inside here before,' Florence observed. 'When I got home from the Crimea, I became a recluse and got ministers to come to me, if they wanted my views on . . . well, the sanitation of India, and suchlike. I generally received them lying in bed. It was quite convenient.'

They ascended to the cabinet-room. Four privileged photographers were waiting. The welcoming functionary went through an inner door. The prime minister appeared, buttoning his jacket.

'Who is it?' he hissed.

'Florence Nightingale, Prime Minister.'

He held out his hand, advancing with a broad smile.

'One more, please, Prime Minister,' requested one of the flashing photographers.

The prime minister disappeared, unbuttoning his jacket.

'What was it like?' Hugo asked, descending the historic stairs.

'Like shaking hands with the Cheshire cat.'

She came in his taxi to St Swithin's. He had private patients to see in the Nightingale block, and he invited her up for a cup of coffee. She stood in the room where they had met. He sat behind the desk.

'I must thank you, Mr Spratt, for all you have done for me.'

'It's nothing, nothing at all.' He smiled. 'You've saved St Swithin's, at least.'

'And I have managed to exert considerable influence, if I may say so, upon the future of the NHS.'

'You have indeed!' he agreed warmly. 'And you've got yourself a career.'

'Unfortunately, I cannot take the position.'

'But you told Bert Goodie you would.'

'One must be polite. Particularly when one has achieved one's goals. I was polite even to the War Office, when I got home from the Crimea. Now I must go.'

He chuckled. 'Back to the Crimea?'

'You could say as much. We shall meet again, Mr Spratt, at a future date. Goodbye.'

She melted into air, into thin air.

Hugo's eyes popped. His jaw dropped. His hands shook.

He rushed from the room, crashing into his secretary with a tray of two coffee cups.

'Sorry! Sorry! Did you see anyone leaving?'

'No, Mr Spratt.'

'Not the . . . the thing I came in with?'

'No, Mr Spratt.'

'I must go to psychiatry.'

'Psychiatry, Mr Spratt?' she questioned, mopping her dress with a tissue.

'I must see my wife. She's pregnant,' he added hastily in explanation.

'Oh, how wonderful!' she said, smiling fondly. 'We always said in the office, children are just what a nice, steady, down-to-earth couple like you need.'

11

FRIDAY WAS WET. In the fashionable Ivy restaurant near Leicester Square, Paula sat at one o'clock with her brief-case under the table and a glass of champagne upon it, in the knowledge that she was about to shatter a clever and amiable man's reputation, career and life.

'What terrible weather!' Professor Whapshott advanced across the crowded restaurant. 'So sorry I'm a little late, Paula. I've only just arrived in London. My Concorde was cancelled, for some inexplicable reason. To do with the coffee machine, I believe. The greatest scientific miracles can trip over twigs. I'd just time to dump my luggage at our Wandsworth flat, and take a shower. Luckily, my wife was at home today. She owns Exquisite Interior Decors. I expect you've heard of them?'

'I'm sure you'd like some champagne?'

'Most certainly. We must identify the gene for jet lag, and remove it from all travellers.' He raised his glass. 'Cheery-ho!'

'Cheers, Professor. How did the lecture tour go?'

'Magnificently.' He fixed her with his bulging eyes. 'The

questions afterwards went on far into the night. And how did my profile go?'

'Let's have something to eat, before we talk about it.'

'I see they have caviar. I had a most rewarding time in Yokohama with Dr Mattakuri, the President of Placenta himself,' he continued with relish. 'The Japanese do entertain so well. One must never refuse anything offered to eat or drink, you know, that is dreadfully bad form. Placenta are doing magnificently at the moment. The have a heart drug wittily called Sumo – I'm sure you get it? – which is being swallowed by almost everyone over fifty in the entire world.'

'After the caviar, perhaps lobster thermidor? They do it very well here.'

'Excellent.'

'Have you any children of your own, Professor?'

'Alas, no. A childless geneticist is like a barefoot cobbler.'

'Have you heard of the two strange babies born to two mothers last year at St Swithin's?'

'There was something in the load of faxes my wife handed me. I haven't looked at them closely yet. From Sir Clarence Strangewood, who's our up-market gynaecologist.'

She let him enjoy his lunch. With the famous sticky toffee pudding, she said, 'Can I tell you a rather disturbing story, Professor?'

'Disturbing?' He looked surprised.

'These two babies I mentioned are identical. Both are males. They are growing up at a rate which is unbelievable. Another few months, and they could take jobs, probably get married.'

She felt in her briefcase.

'Here are the family pictures. As you can see, they have no resemblance whatever to their putative fathers and mothers. These children were not conceived naturally. They were conceived while the mothers were attending an infertility clinic at St Swithin's, the summer before last. Exactly nine months before they gave birth, the pair of them were bitten by two enormous mosquitoes.'

She stopped. She had delivered the sentence. She had tugged the cord of the guillotine, switched on the electric chair, swished the axe. She felt slightly sorry.

Professor Whapshot's cheeks wobbled. His voice had gone. He gulped. He jumped to his feet, and thumped the table with his fist.

'I am the most important man in the world!' he declaimed. 'The most important man in the world!' he emphasized.

He attracted but a few fleeting glances. The *blasé, soigné, épicurien* clientele of the Ivy, being mostly in show business, were undisturbed by outbursts, to which their lives were tediously familiar. Besides, most of them were comfortably convinced that *they* were the most important man in the world.

Paula looked startled. She had expected him to shiver in terror, not jump for joy.

'*Why* are you the most important man in the world?' she enquired.

Professor Whapshott sat down.

'My experiment is an unqualified success. I have created

the perfect human being. I have transformed the human race. Yes, I remember, now. Two of my priceless mosquitoes escaped. Two Adams. I wondered what happened to them, I thought they had perished in a fly-spray. But no. One bite was enough. These two mothers have performed an experiment equivalent to Faraday's discovery of electricity. They must be very, very proud.'

'On the contrary, they are suing St Swithin's for several million pounds.'

He looked blank. 'Why?'

'They want babies that look like them or their husbands, which these babies certainly don't.'

'I think that's being rather pernickety.' He paused, sat back and twiddled his thumbs. 'Well? What happens next?'

'We're running the story on Sunday.'

'Nobody will be particularly interested in a scientific experiment. I've been complaining about that for years.'

'The mothers are getting several more millions for selling it to us.'

'More than Galileo got for discovering the universe,' he observed grouchily.

He finished his coffee and left. At St Swithin's, Sophie and Mandy and their children were waiting in his room. There was a note from Sir Clarence, apologizing that he had to leave because a countess was in labour.

'Well!' said Professor Whapshott.

He sat facing them across the desk, rubbing his hands.

'I've heard the whole story from that journalist you met. I

understand that you are dissatisfied because of no family like-ness with these children?'

He eyed Jeremy and Scott, sucking their dummies and staring at him suspiciously.

'We're devastated,' Sophie enlarged.

'I have the solution. My wife and myself will adopt them.'

'*You* adopt them?' asked Mandy. 'Why?'

'One: because my wife and myself have no children. We'd love to move out of Wandsworth to a nice house in the country, Pinner or somewhere. Your children would be an ideal accompaniment for us. And two: your children repre-sent the pinnacle of my scientific life, one I shall never again scale, however long I live and however hard I work. They would be cherished souvenirs of my professorship here at St Swithin's.'

'Not on your life,' said Mandy.

'They're our babies,' said Sophie, cuddling hers. 'And we want to keep them.'

The professor's brow was contorted in perplexity.

'But you say you don't like them. Because they are not – entirely – your babies. You have made several million pounds telling everybody as much.'

'I gave birth to this baby, and I want to keep him,' stated Sophie, cuddling tighter.

'So do I. I'd rather lose all the millions than lose him,' Mandy proclaimed defiantly, the millions now being safely in the bank (less Terry Boxer's 30% commission).

'Me too,' said Sophie. 'I think.'

'Mind, they're abnormal babies,' the professor admitted. 'They can never be ill. It's not in their genes. And they can never die,' he remembered. 'How does that strike you?'

'It's lovely,' said Mandy. 'I'll wait and see.'

Professor Whapshott shrugged. 'I do not understand women. Not even women's genes.'

There were minders and a limousine waiting outside the hospital. Mandy and Paula with the babies were afforded escape from an increasingly exacting, if profitable, world, to a well-provisioned, well-cellared country house where *Sunday Morning* secreted the people it exploited.

At six o'clock that evening, Hugo sat on the ornate chairman's seat in the St Swithin's committee-room, Sir Lancelot's gall-stone on the long table before him. He was ready to open the bidding.

He was alone.

He was still alone at half-past six.

He picked up the glass case.

'Alas, poor Yorick!' he said solemnly. 'I knew him, Blewett: a fellow of infinite jest, of most excellent fancy: he hath borne me on his back a thousand times; and now, how abhorred in my imagination it is! my gorge rises at it. Here hung those lips that I have kissed I know not how oft. Where be your gibes now? your gambols? your songs? your flashes of merriment, that were wont to set the table in a roar? Not one now, to mock at your own grinning? quite chap-fallen? Now get you to my lady's chamber, and tell her, let her paint an inch thick, to his favour she must come; make her laugh at that.'

He put the case down. What to do with it? A gall-stone would not fit into their decor in Dulwich. He had better return it to the path lab, though they had seemed uncourteously delighted to get rid of it. Perhaps he should drop it into the Thames off London Bridge?

Hugo took the suburban train home. The rush hour was thinning, he could sit in a corner and tear apart the plastic wrapper of that week's *BMJ*.

The first paper inside was depressingly long, even for the *BMJ*. It came from a large team of international physicians and was titled:

CHLORDIOXYMENON CHLORPHENOXYHEPTADINE:

A CLINICAL TRIAL

Practised readers of the *BMJ* read only the paper's summary, printed conveniently at the beginning:

Fifty thousand patients receiving chlordioxymenon chlorphenoxyheptadine ('Sumo') were investigated. The drug was found to be useless.

Oh, well, Hugo thought. My father can go on taking it without noticing any difference.

His eyes strayed to the headline of an evening paper opposite:

JAP DRUG CO SHARES CRASH

He wondered what Alice would be getting for dinner.

The story broke two days later. *Sunday Morning* printed two million extra copies.

THE MOSQUITO BABES stung the world.

Science fiction had caught up with life.

TV turned doomful. Every chat show was chilled with ominous predictions. Two perfectly concocted human beings, loosed upon the earth, induced horrific visions of genetically engineered, identical, men and women marching in crowds along its shopping streets. The pessimists said that this must be prevented by law: the optimists, that we should probably get used to it. A rapid telephone poll of viewers found only 2% in favour, and they, as upon similar intrusions, thought they were being asked about something else.

Everybody agreed that these perilous and reckless geneticists should be scientifically emasculated. The first would be Professor Whapshott, whose name had become as familiar by Sunday lunchtime as Guy Fawkes.

The professor could not understand it at all. He passed Sunday in his Wandsworth flat, besieged by reporters; he stayed in bed and gave out that he was suffering from recrudescent smallpox.

In the House of Commons that Tuesday, Bert Goodie fought off scary questions from MPs on both sides (already vaguely speculating which way these manufactured voters would turn). The minister was content to make a single point: it was not his fault. The culprit was St Swithin's Hospital. He was closing it down after Christmas.

At Question Time on Wednesday, the prime minister responded to fierce probing about his handling of this crisis for the human race.

'Crisis? What crisis? These are little local difficulties in a genetics laboratory. It doesn't mean, of course, that these genes in your chromosomes have been devalued.'

The pope seemed about to send for the Inquisition. The Archbishop of Canterbury said that all English churches would be fumigated against mosquitoes.

The porters shut the great gate of St Swithin's against an intrusive mob, the first occasion since the body-snatching riots of 1820. Professor Whapshott sat all day in his white coat in his office, his scientific brain numbed. His only way to commute to Wandsworth was by ambulance, into which he was inserted on a stretcher, with his face hidden under a blanket, like a corpse.

A week after his Friday luncheon with Paula, the imprisoned professor was eating an egg sandwich and drinking a light ale, brought by Jiang to his desk, when an assistant from the laboratory announced that Dr Mattakuri had arrived to see him.

Professor Whapshott was astounded. The President of Placenta himself, who had the pharmaceutics of the entire world under his hyper-efficient control, and from whom he had parted so cordially ten days ago, had come specially from Yokohama to inspect his laboratory.

Dr Mattakuri was short and slight, with thick black hair and thick glasses, dressed in a faultlessly smooth dark suit.

He carried a briefcase. He bowed.

'Professor Whapshott,' he said, still standing. 'I come in person for two reasons. First: all is finished.'

'What's finished?' asked Professor Whapshott curiously.

'All this.' The Japanese made a slight gesture. 'Your laboratory.'

'But you can't close it down.' The professor looked lost. 'Several of my important experiments are just coming to completion.'

'We have no money for it.'

'No money? I can't believe it!'

'We have no money for anything. We are bankrupt. Broke. *Kaputt. C'est fini. Grazie e arrivederia,*' he said, exhibiting the global adaptability of the Japanese.

'But how did that happen? You're one of the biggest firms in the world. Bigger even than the fashionable computers.'

'Sumo,' Dr Mattakuri replied simply. 'It has been proved useless. No one will buy it any more. This is always happening in the drug industry. Market an effective drug for stomach disease, someone else markets a better one, your shares plummet. Market an ineffective drug, and you are in the *suupu*, as you English say. Now: I have something more important. This is so serious, that I have come from Yokohama personally to tell you.'

'What could there be more important than closing my lab?' asked the professor despairingly.

'You have done genetic engineering on mosquitoes. That was not in your contract.'

The professor shrugged. 'It was a little diversion of my own. Surely your employees are allowed a hobby?'

'It is something that has appalled the world. Human life is a gift of Buddha. You bestowed it yourself. To take over the functions of Buddha is an outrage. While employed by a Japanese company. It is bad public relations. Both for our company, which is eclipsed, and for our country, which is the ever-rising sun. We have enough trouble with our image as it is, since the last war.'

'But I only wanted to *know* how to do it,' the professor protested. 'I didn't want to *do* it.'

Dr Mattakuri opened his briefcase and handed the professor a curved metal sheath.

'What's that?'

'A sword. *Hara-kiri.* You commit, please. Soon. Good afternoon.'

He bowed and left.

Professor Whapshott drew the ivory-handled weapon from its decorated silver. He gingerly tried it. Sharp as a scalpel. His eyes roved, his forehead knotted, his cheeks shook. He threw the suicide tool on the floor. He went next door to the animal room. Jiang had gone. He threw up the window. He seized the cages now crammed tightly with buzzing mosquitoes. For a few seconds, he fondly stroked the mesh. He opened the tops. The mosquitoes flew instantly into the delightful damp and warm air.

'They will breed perfectly, in these conditions,' Professor Whapshott muttered fiercely. 'Mosquito control in Britain is negligible. Each Adam and Eve are now copulating like mad. A couple of days, and each female will lay three hundred eggs. Which will shortly become three hundred times three hundred eggs, with another generation, and so on, and so on. Each mosquito will sting a human female, who will become pregnant. Fly, fly! I have created another human race! Homo Whapshott! A race which will never be ill! A race which will live for ever! For ever and ever! You lucky people! I hope you all find enough room. Oh, how clever I am! I have the last laugh!'

He began to laugh. He laughed all his way through the lab. He laughed maniacally across the St Swithin's courtyard, waving his arms in the air. He screamed with laughter through the great gate, and disappeared into the London crowd, unaware of what was in store for them.

On a Monday morning the following March, Hugo and Alice were reclining on the beach at Barbados. It was getting on for lunch.

They had decided on Barbados, as more convenient than the Seychelles. The island's sands around them were as uncontaminated with human footprints as were Robinson Crusoe's. The Atlantic Ocean in front glittered in the unrelenting sunlight, and broke with majestic laziness on the shore. The white-walled, green-roofed villa they had rented, isolated from the tourist mob, was priced as a retreat for millionaires. But that was of no consequence.

By touching his stockbroker friend in Poultry, Hugo had raised the Spratt Scholarship fund by a few thousands. But, as

Amanda had indicated in the students' bar, this was barely enough to keep, over the years, modern scholars, who were not content to study unsupped by candlelight in a freezing attic.

After some thought, Hugo had changed his prospectus to the Spratt Sabbatical. Some bright member of the St Swithin's staff would enjoy a year's experience at some distant university hospital, an education for them both. Then it occurred to him that the sum needed for the maintenance of a medical fellow at Columbia or McGill University, or at Moscow or Beijing, would outstrip the resources. So why not a Spratt Vacation, he considered, for overstressed St Swithin's consultants?

There was money enough only for one decent hols, he decided generously, and as its bestowal was in his exclusive power, he awarded it to himself.

Alice had been urging him for months to take a period of far-away tranquillity, to preserve his sanity. He was wondering still if Florence Nightingale and St Lancelot were heavenly spirits, or his unquiet fantasies. He supposed that Hamlet in Elsinore must have pondered the same.

Up in the villa, the perfect one-month-old Lancelot Peregrine Spratt slept in his basket. He was the final baby to be born in St Swithin's, before it was shut and its truncated functions merged with St Bartholomew's Hospital, 'Bart's', round the corner in Smithfield, with which had passed several centuries of intense rivalry in the groves of Academe and on the fields of sport.

In the disorganization of moving, everybody had forgotten about the Spratt Memorial. And if anyone had noticed that Hugo had pocketed it, they would have considered it had reached a deserving destination.

Hugo and Alice sat on loungers under bright umbrellas. She was wearing a black two-piece swimsuit, knitting little white things. He was in scarlet shorts, reading *The War of the Worlds* by H.G. Wells, a novelist in whom he had recently developed an intense interest. He was sipping a tall glass of iced rum and coke. George the Bajan butler, in white jacket with napkin over forearm, descended the slope from the veranda with a tray.

'Yesterday's London paper has just arrived, madam.'

'Oh, thank you.'

Alice unfolded *Sunday Morning*.

MOSQUITO BABES ARE BACK

ran the headline. The front page continued:

TWENTY LONDON MOTHERS GET SAME BABIES.

'Look!' she exclaimed.

Hugo put a finger on his place in the paperback, and idly turned his head.

Alice continued keenly: 'It says that these mothers had babies precisely like the ones born to that troublesome couple – remember? I forget their names now. With poor Professor

Whapshott, before they had to take him away. Their two children's pictures are always in the papers, getting up to something. Five of this new lot were born in Bart's. That's going to set them back a bit.'

She read on: 'There's reports of others, exactly the same sort of babies, born last Saturday in Norwich, Edinburgh, Paris and Brussels, and Ajaccio, for some reason. By today,' she prognosticated, 'they'll be popping out in New York and Sydney and Tokyo. You can't keep mosquitoes out of aeroplanes. How fortunate, with little Lancelot, that we jumped the gun.'

Alice folded the paper on her lap.

'Hugo, dearest,' she pronounced solemnly. 'This is the end of the human race as we know it. What have you to say to that?'

'George!'

'Sir?'

'Bring me another rum and coke, please. Same amount of ice. But rather more rum.'

'Very good, sir.'